ABOUT THE AUTHOR

Joyee Flynn grew up in Chicago, living in the same house all her life until she went left for college. Though she has a great life, she loves to get lost in fantasy that only books can bring. Her wide interest in reading is reflected in her writings. Currently, Joyee lives with her dog, Marius, named after a vampire from Anne Rice's *Interview with the Vampire* series. She dreams of one day living out in Montana, with enough land to have a few horses, and find a couple of cowboys of her own.

A lover of men, Joyee's all about them in any form in her books. Vampire, werewolf, military, doesn't matter at all as long as they are hot, hard, and sex fiends!

WWW.JOYEEFLYNN.COM

LUST & FAE

ANYTHING GOES, BOOK ONE

JOYEE FLYNN

SILVERPUBLISHING
Published by Silver Publishing
Publisher of Erotic Romance

﴾SILVERPUBLISHING

ISBN 978-1456549015

Lust and Fae

Visit Silver Publishing at www.SilverPublishing.info

DEDICATION

To Reese:

For always putting up with my crazy ideas and wants for
our covers.
Man-shopping with you for cover models is like the
highlight of my month!
You're crazy talented, girl,
and I'm so grateful you're the one who makes my ideas and
books come to life.

CHAPTER 1

Scanning the crowd I saw exactly what I needed, someone looking for lust. Granted, my club was full of them, but when I'm hungry I don't want just anyone. That was part of the reason we opened the club, to have hundreds of options every night. Like normal clubs, we had a variety of different people from all walks of life. Some were locals who came regularly to find a warm body for their bed; others were here on vacation and wanted to live it up.

The hot twink I had my eyes on had recently suffered a loss and wanted nothing but to forget and feel something pleasurable. I loved the way he moved his slim hips and tight ass. He couldn't have been more than twenty-five and seemed to know the scene. His jeans were low cut and tight, and his upper half was bare. He looked up just then, as if sensing me, and when he saw the crook of my finger, he made his way through the crowd.

"Hello," he purred as he threw his arms around my neck. I knew it was my eternal beauty he saw and my essence that had him on me without any reservations or hesitation. At about six-five and two-twenty of lean muscle, I knew what I looked like to the people that showed up looking for a night off from their lives.

"You want to suck my cock, don't you?" I asked, moving us back towards the bar. The twink nodded rapidly as he ran his hands over my chest. I sat on one of the bar stools and another man caught my eye. He wanted to stop living a lie and finally touch another man. I crooked my finger at the burly guy, and I read his mind, finding out his name was Mike. "And Mike wants to fuck your ass while you do it."

"Oh hell yeah," the smaller man replied as he looked at Mike. The big guy immediately walked the ten feet between us and took the twink into his arms. Mike was about my size, with blond hair to my black, and green eyes to my blue. I found his muscular physique quite alluring. Watching them kiss with no inhibitions was great, really got me going. But for me to feed, I had to be part of it. I reached out and touched the twink, who immediately broke from the kiss and started undoing his pants.

"Slick up your fingers and stretch him out so you don't hurt him," I instructed Mike, tossing him the small tube of slick I always kept in my pocket. Couldn't be a lust demon and not be prepared. Yeah, me and all the other good scouts.

I glanced around as they were getting ready for fun. One would think a ménage at the bar of a packed club wouldn't be allowed. They'd be wrong. It was not only allowed, it was encouraged. And we weren't the only ones. But when I was involved, it drew a lot of attention. It came with the territory of being a demon, especially a lust demon.

"Can I please suck you now?" the hot little twink asked me as he eyed my groin. His jeans were hanging around his ankles, leaving him naked and he had so much lust in his eyes it made me shiver. Not breaking his gaze, I unzipped my fly and let my cock free. He glanced up at me as if asking again, and with my nod, he leaned over and licked my cock. "You taste like homemade apple pie."

"Then eat me up, just no chewing," I said, gently pushing his head back down. He braced his hands on my thighs as he took the head of my dick into his mouth. While I knew the twink didn't have much experience, he made up for it with his enthusiasm. Mike had been busy getting him ready. I watched as the big guy pushed a third finger in the smaller man's ass. I reached out and touched Mike. "It's time for you to live as you are. Don't you think?"

"Yes, yes I do," Mike answered, pulling his fingers from the twink's ass. He unzipped his jeans, pulled out a monstrous cock, and slicked it up. We'd grown quite a crowd now, and some of the bouncers appeared to help hold people off. If any of them touched us while we played, they'd be helpless to stop themselves from joining in. Our boys knew to intercede so we didn't have a chain gang fucking line going across the club.

"Is this what you've always wanted?" I asked Mike, bliss written all over his face. He nodded, his eyes still closed as he savored the feeling of pushing into the twink. I watched the gentle giant take great care with the smaller man under him. Mike never pushed too hard, taking his time until the ass he wanted opened for him.

"Better than I ever imagined," Mike panted, trying to control his need to thrust the rest of the way. I watched the man control himself, slowly working in that third leg of a dick until he was finally seated. Mike leaned over and whispered in the man's ear, "You were made for me. I will never hurt you, baby."

The twink moaned loudly around my cock as he pulled me forward then impaled himself on Mike's cock. The large man got the idea and started fucking the firm ass in front of him. The lust I was getting off them both was like a continuous tidal wave. I hadn't fed this well in weeks. And no, I wasn't taking their souls or any shit like that. Vampires need blood to survive, and I need lust.

"Smack his sweet ass," I told Mike, seeing the twink's deepest desires. Mike's eyes went wide as a feral smile crossed his face. He raised his large hand and spanked the smaller man while he pounded into his ass.

The little guy went wild, sucking me down as far as he could as he fondled my sac. "Harder, Mike. He wants it harder."

"Fuck yes." Mike hissed as I watched his control snap. He thrust so hard and fast into the man that the twink was pushed up and down on my cock with the movement. Running my fingers through his hair, I kept him from choking himself on my dick.

"Touch his cock." I moaned, loving the hot mouth wrapped around my favorite body part. Mike reached down, and I could feel how much he loved stroking the smaller man's dick. The twink cried out, shooting his load all over the floor. Mike growled, his nostrils flaring with desire as he followed into orgasmic pleasure as well. Now that they had both come, I was free to. Holding the small man's head to me, I felt my cock explode and shoot stream after stream of cum down his throat.

When I was finished, the man moved his mouth off me and laid his head down on my thigh. He smiled up at me, and I gave him a wink. Mike slumped to his knees, taking the twink with him.

"Is it always like that?" Mike asked, panting as he cradled the man to him.

"No, it's not. This man is perfect, I wouldn't let him get away," I answered, seeing that they both desperately wanted to love and be loved. I bent over, giving them both a quick kiss. "And your cock is fantastic, he'd be an idiot to ever give that up."

"Would you really want me again?" the twink asked, staring up at Mike, eyes wide.

"Oh yeah, I think you should always be attached to my dick," Mike replied before kissing him. I watched for a moment as the two men clung to each other while playing tonsil hockey.

"You always were a sap, Cal." Eaton snickered as he appeared beside me. He was almost my double in looks, except he had an inch on me and one of those proud Roman noses. "I've never known a lust demon who matched up so many couples."

"Just because I feed off lust doesn't make me evil or not believe in love," I growled. He'd hit a sensitive issue for me, but it wouldn't do much good to lose my cool with him. Eaton had been a good friend over the centuries and an even better partner in the club.

There were five of us lust demons that started up *Anything Goes* a few years ago. We'd set up on the outskirts of Sin City. I mean, what better place for everyone and anyone to engage in their wildest fantasies if not Las Vegas?

The club we designed from the ground up. The first

floor was the main dance floor and bars, with elevated stages every so often for performers to dance or strip on. Occasionally we had an over zealous guest who jumped up and tried their skills on the stripper pole. But normally we had pros that people could enjoy.

Three quarters of the main floor had booths on the outskirts. Anyone could have one of the booths and do anything they wished. Several couples and threesomes were having their fun at any given time, being entertainment for those who liked to watch.

Not being on the strip kept those who just wanted to ogle from walking in. But the people who wanted serious fun made the trip from their hotels to enjoy a night they'd never forget. My partners in the club and I weren't bad demons; we didn't force people to do things they didn't want to. We simply took away the inhibitions and let people feel free to do what they wanted without pressure.

We were able to get some wrath demons to work as security and doormen, which worked out well for them since they fed on anger. It helped us because, when wrath demons fed, it drained the human of their anger. So they were motivated to get involved in any squabble since it kept them well fed. We also paid them, but it was really the constant aggression you could find at a sex club that kept the wrath demons loyal employees.

"Don't you think it ruins our reputations a bit if you use your abilities to help desperate fools?" Eaton asked as we walked up to the private elevators to our offices.

"This coming from the man who has a very large collection of chick flicks." I smirked, throwing his secret in his face.

"Cal, you can't tell anyone about that," he begged, going pale. "I'm sorry, I won't pick on you anymore, okay?"

"Deal," I replied as we walked onto the elevator and I scanned the keycard that allowed it to move. The doors swooshed closed and up to the third floor we went. The second floor consisted mainly of private balconies that needed to be reserved. There were also sections where anyone could just stand and watch the overview of the goings on below.

"Harder! Fuck me harder," Mick, one of my other partners, screamed as the doors opened. His latest boy toy submissive was pounding into Mick so hard I was surprised the table hadn't collapsed yet. While most demons were larger in height and frame, Mick was about five-six and a hundred and thirty pounds.

"I need to get laid," Eaton grumbled as he rubbed his hand over his growing erection. I couldn't blame him; the scene in front of us was hot. Mick was on his back on the conference table we had in the suite of offices. His legs were up in the air, spread wide by boy toy, as his ass was fucked mercilessly. "They started before you did downstairs. I left to remind you of the meeting."

"They've been going at it this whole time?" I asked, raising an eyebrow as we stepped closer. I knew we couldn't orgasm until our partners did; it ensured we got the maximum amount of lust possible to feed from.

"You may come, baby," Mick grunted. The large man fucking him cried out his release as if Mick had flipped some invisible switch on him. Mick's new toy was definitely a hot piece, with dark auburn hair and not an inch of fat on him. I'd guess he was maybe six-two and one-eighty-five or so. I watched as the muscles in the man's ass, back, and shoulders twitched and flexed as his body was overcome with his climax. Shaking my head, I walked to my office.

The main room contained a sitting area, conference room table, and a kitchen. We'd chosen shades of lighter, warm colors up here to contrast the vivid blues and greens downstairs. Then there were six offices in a semicircle along the walls. That way, we could all see down into the club if we needed to. The best part was the small balconies coming off each office. Eaton was quite the exhibitionist and thought to put them in. I was forever grateful he had, having used mine often for my fun.

As I entered my office, I heard Mick scream, and knew he'd gotten off. I plopped down in my plush desk chair behind the huge oak desk, put my feet up, and waited for everyone else to join us. Each office was about the size of most studio apartments, with their own sitting areas. Eaton took a seat in one of the couches, still watching the show in the main area through the still open door.

"I think I need to borrow Mick's new toy," Temp said as he walked quickly in. Temp was on the opposite side of the spectrum from Mick, coming in at six-eight and over three hundred pounds. They weren't really our names, I mean what kind of name was Temp for a demon? We'd shorted most of our god awful names into something that fit better into society. "He can go for hours, trained as a real submissive who can't come unless you order him to."

"Would you like to play with Temp, baby?" Mick asked his new boy as he was carried into the office.

"If it would please you, my one and only," the man answered as he lowered Mick to his feet.

"Everyone, this is Alex. Alex, these are my partners," Mick said, introducing everyone. "And we'll see if you're good, then maybe I'll let you play with Temp."

"Thank you, my one and only," Alex replied, kneeling at Mick's feet.

"Did you forget something, Alex?" Mick asked, his

tone disapproving. When Alex looked up at him with confusion, Mick raised an eyebrow and pointed to his ass. "I don't like feeling dirty, Alex."

"I'm sorry, I was waiting for your order to do so," Alex begged, reaching for Mick. "Am I to always immediately clean you after our lovemaking?"

"Yes, unless I tell you otherwise, baby," Mick answered, his features softening. "I didn't tell you that yet, I apologize for getting mad. Clean me up well and I promise you rewards tonight."

"Thank you, my love." Alex sighed, visibly relieved. He moved behind Mick, and I had a fantastic view of Alex's huge tongue licking his own cum out of Mick's ass.

"His tongue, it's quiet large," I said, getting incredibly hard.

"My new baby is a tiger shifter," Mick replied, then moaned as Alex spread the cheeks of his ass. "He's very oral and loves the taste of cum, even his own if he licks it out of me."

"Oh fuck," Temp groaned and rubbed his groin. "Think he could take all of us?"

"If he's very, very good, I might allow him to play. But I'm not inclined to share him as I did my previous toys," Mick replied, and for a second, I saw Mick smile before he schooled his features. "I plan on keeping him very busy most of the time."

"You're the only Dom I know who likes to be the bottom." Sark chuckled as he joined us. "Sorry I'm late, but we had quite as uprising after your little show on the floor, Cal."

"I aim to please," I replied, smiling widely. I gestured to Alex who was moaning as he enthusiastically ate Mick's ass. "I don't seem to be the only one."

"You always find the best boys, Mick. How do you do it?" Sark asked as he sat down.

"Just because they're big and built doesn't mean they don't want a firm hand," Mick answered. "And some don't like men stronger than themselves; they like us twink-looking men. But I give as good as I take, and that's why they're loyal to me. Isn't that right, baby?"

"Yes, my love. You have treated me better than any master I have ever had," Alex answered, finishing up his task. He moved around Mick, still kneeling and licked Mick's cum off his stomach.

"What have I told you about that word, Alex? You know how it offends me that you think of me as your master."

"No, I don't think of you that way. I swear, my one and only," Alex stuttered. I watched his back muscles shake as he grabbed Mick's hips. "I was simply saying you are a god compared to the way other doms have treated me in the past. I did not mean you were my master, I know you hate the term."

Mick studied the man for several moments, causing Alex to shake even harder. "Alright, baby. I believe you."

"Thank you, my love," Alex said, nestling his face in Mick's groin. "I would never forgive myself if I ever hurt or offended you."

"You haven't," Mick replied, stroking Alex's face, again giving us a glimpse into his softer side. "I'd like to sit down now, Alex."

"Yes, my love." Alex purred, immediately standing before sitting on one of the couches, pulling Mick onto his lap. They definitely had one of the strangest D/s relationships I'd ever seen, but they both seemed happy. Now that Mick was clean and seated, he clothed them with a flick of his wrist. One of the neat tricks we enjoy as demons. It didn't seem to stop Alex's attention to Mick, running his hands all over the smaller man's body.

"Okay, that was fun to watch, but I called this meeting for a reason," I said, clearing my throat to get everyone's attention. It was difficult at times when you had five lust demons in one room to get them to focus. Well, and a really hot piece of man candy with a huge tongue.

"Yeah, so what's the big emergency meeting about?" Eaton asked as he turned his attention back to me.

"Beck said there were some halfers trying to sneak in tonight," I answered, everyone going quiet and tense. Beck was our head of security and probably the most hard-core, badass wrath demon I'd ever met. Halfers, as full blood demons called them, were demons who were once human. They had died, gone to hell, and lost whatever humanity they ever possessed. Halfers were the soulless demons most horror movies and books were based on.

Lust demons, on the other hand, were born this way, as angels were. And as there are seven castes of demons, what humans referred to as the seven deadly sins, the same exists with angels.

"Did they get anyone from the club?" Sark asked, leaning forward and resting his forearms on his knees. Halfers were unable to feel any emotion, unless they found someone who came in contact with a full blood demon. If a halfer fucked the twink or Mike after I did earlier, he would feel all our lust. And to someone who was once human and no longer felt anything, that meant a lot to them. The lengths they were willing to go to feel were impressive.

"No, Beck spotted them right away," I answered, shaking my head. "The problem was there were four of them together. Normally they're loners, so these ones are different for whatever reason. I thought it was something everyone needed to know."

"I agree," Temp replied, running his fingers through his hair. "Beck's been trying to get some more wrath demons here for the new club. I think until we know what's going on, we should have a few more outside watching the parking lots and people leaving. It would be really bad if people started disappearing when they left here."

"Plus, we've closed the deal on the new location," Mick added, moving Alex's hands to his sides so he wasn't distracted. Alex took it in stride, closing his eyes and resting now that he'd been dismissed. "I mean, I don't want anyone to get hurt, I care about that. It's just that finding the perfect location for our next club has been a headache; I don't want anything to mess this up."

"We know you're not a rat bastard, Mick," I replied, glancing around. "Okay, so we all agree about adding more security until we know what's going on?"

"Yeah, but I think we should also keep the public sex shows with strangers to a minimum until we get this handled," Sark said. "I think that will help with eyes we might not be able to keep out of the club."

"Agreed," I answered when I saw the other nodding. Though it was a good plan, it didn't seem to relieve the concern I saw on the faces of my friends. If halfers were starting to band together, we could have a lot bigger problems than a few of our leftovers being used by them.

CHAPTER 2

The next night I was leaning on the rail of the balcony connected to my office, watching a fascinating show below. If I had any inkling to ever touch a woman, the one going at it with four guys would have been the one I chose. She was gorgeous and very gifted. One cock in her pussy, one in her ass, while sucking another one, and giving a fourth guy a hand job. Once people lost their inhibitions at the door, things like this happened frequently. Like the wonderful accountant taking on four men as I was watching.

A small glimmer caught my eye by the entrance. Glancing over, I did a double take when I saw a single fae was here.

Fuck! I growled in my head as I raced to the elevator. Pushing the button for the ground floor, I tapped my foot impatiently as I waited. As soon as the doors opened, I was out of there like a shot. I made my way through the crowd, most of them giving me a lust-filled glance as I brushed past them.

"No fae are allowed in here," I said as I grabbed the small man's arm and saw he was breathtaking. He was about five-five and a hundred twenty-five pounds of lean, hot man. His short blond, almost white curls and deep lavender eyes were so alluring, anyone would gladly trade everything they owned for one night with him. Touching him gave me all sorts of readings into his head. "Especially *virgin* fae. You'll throw the club into complete chaos and get hurt."

"My name is Gabe," a soft voice said; it was almost musical. But then, fae were more alluring than even demons were. "Not Fae."

"You're kidding, right?" I asked, pulling him towards the door. "I know what you are, kid."

"Please don't make me go back out there," Gabe begged, trying to get away. "I came in here to hide; someone's following me."

"Yeah, right," I replied as we walked back through the doors. It was early on a Sunday night, so for once, there wasn't a line at the door. As we passed the bouncer, I gestured to the man I was holding onto. "What were you thinking, letting fae in?"

"Sorry, Cal, I didn't know. I've never seen a fairy before," he answered, squirming under my gaze. I realized it was one of the new guys and calmed down.

"Just because I'm gay does not make me a fairy," Gabe yelled, tugging his arm away from me. "And I think it's very mean of you to say so. I came to find you, Cal."

I shared a look with the wrath demon, who simply

gave me a shrug. Turning back to the fae, I saw several halfers approaching us. In a flash I moved him front of Gabe, holding him behind me.

"Tell Beck we have a code six and take Gabe to Mick. He's working the bar," I growled, pushing the fae towards him. Focusing back on the halfers, one seemed to be leading the rest. "What are you doing here? You know who we are and what we can do to you."

"There's just one of you." The halfer snickered. "Give us the fairy and we'll leave, no violence. All we want is the fae."

"Why? The fae don't have any powers that can help you. You had your chance to have a good afterlife, and you blew it," I yelled, feeling very protective over the little fae for some reason. And a little guilty that I hadn't believed him.

"Give us the fae or we'll destroy your club and everyone inside it," the halfer said calmly, but I could see the anger in his eyes and knew I'd gotten to him. Halfers were horrible to look at, their bodies and faces twisted with their sins.

"Not going to happen, halfer," I answered, seeing my crew coming out to back me up. "And it's not just me here. We've always got lots of demons around. Still think you can take us?"

"Oh yeah," the halfer answered, and I saw lots more of them step out of the shadows. Before I could even answer, they started to rush us, which was stupid on their part. Full-blood demons had lots of powers they didn't. Lust demons controlled fire, and wrath demons wielded ice.

Mick was the first to unleash his fire, flames shooting out of his hands at the closest halfers. The rest of us joined in. Though we couldn't kill them, if we burnt them crispy, their essence or whatever they were made up of would be sent back to hell. After we'd fried several of them, the rest started to turn tail and run.

Beck and his guys stepped up then, putting out the residual fires. Beck was about Temp's size, but even wider in the shoulders.

"We'll clean this up," Beck said, giving us a nod as he went back to icing our fires.

"Thanks, Beck," Mick replied as we turned and headed inside.

"Where's the fae?" I asked him.

"I had one of the wrath guys watch him behind the bar," Mick explained as we walked through the entrance. "You know I never miss a fight."

"Gabe," I said softly, rushing towards the bar. Something inside of me needed to see he was alright with my own eyes. I saw him huddled in the corner behind the bar. "Gabe, it's okay now. They're gone."

"What were those things?" he asked, eyes wide and darting around. "Why did they want me?"

"I don't know, but you're under our protection now," I answered, holding my arms out to him. Gabe seemed to think a moment before launching himself into my embrace. I tried to ignore the fact that he fit perfectly and it felt right to hold him. "We'll figure this out, baby."

"I should be mad at you for calling me a fairy," he giggled, wiping his eyes. He snuggled closer to me as I stood, wrapping his arms around my neck. I moved his legs over my waist as I made my way towards the elevators. Temp raised an eyebrow at me as he held the door until I was inside with them.

"Gabe, it wasn't a slam on your sexuality," I whispered in his ear. "I'm gay too, we all are in this elevator. It's what you are; you're fae."

"I'm human," he replied, leaning back so he could look me in the face. I saw he didn't seem as convinced as he had earlier. "Aren't I?"

"No, little one, you're very much a fae," Temp ground out, causing me to glance at him. He and my other partners were holding themselves back as if they were having trouble with their control. When they elevator doors opened, they immediately rushed out as if they needed air.

"What's with you guys?" I asked, completely shocked as to how they were acting.

"How are you staying in control, Cal?" Eaton asked me, holding onto the conference table. "I'm having trouble not throwing the fae down and fucking him into the floor."

"Guys, we've had fairies here before," I answered slowly. There were a few stripper fairies we hired as entertainment at the club once a month. We had to be very careful, having extra security around, since the fae were alluring to humans. Actually, they were alluring to pretty much anything with a pulse, but humans didn't understand why they were drawn to them.

"Please don't let them rape me," Gabe said softly, holding onto me for dear life. "I thought they were your friends."

"They are, Gabe. They won't hurt you," I replied, staring at my four friends as I hugged him close. "I don't get what's going on with you guys."

"He's a virgin, isn't he?" Temp asked, racing around the other side of the large table. "That's why we are having trouble. Virgin fae are even more tempting and alluring than regular fairies."

"How did you know?" Gabe replied, his eyes going wide as he turned to look at them. "I've been promised to Cal."

"Alex!" Mick yelled, his boy appearing out of his office instantly. Alex's eyes went wide as he moved towards us as if in a trance. "No, Alex! You can't have the fae."

"But I want him." Alex whimpered as Mick dragged the shifter back into his office.

"No, but you're going to fuck me right now," Mick growled, slamming the door behind them.

"Can someone call Alejandro? We need to get this figured out," I said, slowly walking towards my office. Everyone's eyes followed us, as if they were stalking their prey. "Guys, snap out of it! We need help here. Why were the halfers after this fae?"

"Right, I'm on it," Eaton answered, snapping out of it first. "I'll tell him to appear in your office."

"Thanks," I replied before closing the door to my office so Gabe and I were alone.

"How come you don't seem to want me?" Gabe whispered into my neck. He couldn't be more wrong, because I wanted him more than I'd ever wanted any being in all my existence.

"I do want you, Gabe. But I'm a lust demon; virgins don't really fit with us," I answered carefully.

"Lust demon? Is that why I want you so badly?" he asked, his hands roaming over my shoulders.

"Probably," I replied, sad for the first time that someone wanted me for being a demon. I'd never felt that before, this desire for Gabe to want me because I was Cal, not a lust demon. "Eaton is calling in a fairy we know; he'll help us figure this out."

"But I want to stay with you," Gabe answered, rubbing his hips over my stomach.

"Gabe, you have to behave or you won't be a virgin much longer." I groaned, holding him still.

"I want you to take me," he purred, kissing my neck. "I've never wanted anyone ever, Cal. But I want you."

"I can't, Gabe," I said, pulling him off of me and setting him on his feet. "You're too innocent to be involved with me or my world."

"That's where you'd be wrong, Cal," Alejandro replied, appearing in front of us. He had all the typical fae features, very lean with blond hair and striking eyes. The only difference is he was taller than any fairy I'd ever met. I instinctively pushed Gabe behind me as if to protect him. "Gabe is your charge."

"What does that mean?" I asked, suddenly needing to sit down. I grabbed one of the chairs and collapsed in it. Pulling Gabe with me, onto my lap.

"Wow, you're gorgeous." Gabe whispered, eyeing over Alejandro.

"So are you, sprite," Alejandro replied. "Gabe is an orphan. He didn't even know he was fae until you told him, Cal."

"I got that part," I said, holding Gabe against my chest. "Why did the halfers want him so badly?"

"If a halfer is involved with a fae's first time, they can regain their humanity," Alejandro explained, sitting across from us. "I believe they want him for what you would call a 'gang bang'. They all take turns with Gabe, and since it would still technically all be his first time, all of them would regain what they had lost. But this cannot happen."

"Of course not! I won't let them rape Gabe," I exclaimed, securely wrapping my arms around the smaller man.

"Not only that, but they would take away Gabe's essence and make him mortal," Alejandro replied. "Gabe is a sprite, a very rare fae. That's why, when his parents died, we opted to hide him amongst trusted humans."

"Is that why the convent was attacked?" Gabe asked, tears in his eyes. Great, not only was he a virgin, but he grew up around nuns.

"Tell me what happened, sprite," Alejandro ordered, none too gently, getting a growl from me in response. Alejandro smiled widely at me. "And that would be why you are his guardian."

"What does that mean?"

"First, I need to know what happened to Gabe," he answered, his tone more gentle this time. "Please tell me how you got here, little one."

"Sister Catherine woke me in the middle of the night," Gabe started to say, shaking in my arms. Without a thought, I rubbed my hands over him, trying to soothe his nerves. "She told me to get dressed quickly and handed me an envelope. It had lots of money in it and an ID for me. She said to go find Cal in Vegas, that he was who would protect me now. We snuck out a back entrance of the convent, and she drove me to a train station. She told me to talk to no one but Cal, and there were instructions on how to find him."

"You came here for me?" I asked, looking from Gabe to Alejandro. "Why? I'm a lust demon; do you know what that means?"

"It means you are the perfect protector and mate for a sprite," Alejandro answered. "They need a lot more from a mate than most fae. Sprites are very rare and precious, Cal."

"Demons don't mate, Alejandro," I said, narrowing my eyes at him. "And you know how I feed! How can I have a mate and fuck others? That's not right."

"Would I get to watch?" Gabe asked, drawing my attention back to him. The look on his face full of heat and desire.

"And now you understand why he's perfect for you." Alejandro chuckled, confusing me even more. "Sprites are very much into sharing and watching. You cannot feed off his lust, so you will have to continue with others. The other difference is sprites can have children whether they are male or female."

"You want me to get him pregnant?" I gasped. I hadn't missed the part of Gabe wanting to watch me with someone else, the idea got my hard. But knocking him up? That was a new one, even for me. "Demons can't reproduce."

"Yes they can, if they are given a mate," Alejandro replied gently. "I know this is a lot to take in, but you were specially chosen, Cal. You're not an evil demon; you are one of the kindest demons I've ever met, my friend. That's why you were given such a gift."

"By who?" I asked, raising an eyebrow.

"Way above my pay grade." He chuckled. "As soon as you take his virginity, your friends will calm down and see him as a normal fae. It will also protect him from the halfers. They want him for his virginity. After he loses it, they will no longer seek him out and will stay far away.

Sprites are also the strongest of all of us, able to kill halfers, not just send them back to hell."

"Fuck," I answered, my eyes going wide. I groaned when I felt Gabe's smaller hand unbutton the top of my shirt and run his fingers over my chest.

"I'll leave you two to get acquainted," Alejandro said, standing. "If you have more questions, you know how to reach me."

"Wait, what about this offspring?" I asked, holding Gabe's hand still.

"You will have many sprites, but they will have some of your powers as well," he answered. "They will not be part demon if that's what you are worried about."

"Part of it," I replied honestly. "What if I can't do this, Alejandro? Look at my life. Do you think this is a place for an innocent fae and children?"

"It's perfect actually." Alejandro chuckled. "Get to know Gabe and you will see why. If you need me call me, otherwise I expect to hear from you as soon as he starts having morning sickness."

"Wait, I've not agreed to this," I growled, standing as I set Gabe onto his feet.

"You don't want me?" Gabe asked quietly, his eyes filing up with tears.

"No, baby, I'm not saying that at all," I answered,

leaning over to kiss his forehead. "I just don't think I can subject you to my life."

Glancing back at Alejandro, I saw he'd already vanished. *Asshole*, I thought to myself.

"But I'm yours, Cal. I've always known I'm yours," Gabe told me. "I knew I wasn't a normal human, but the sisters never told me I was fae. They prepared me for the day I would be with you. I was scared at the idea of belonging to a stranger I would have to please, but meeting you, it's all I want to do."

"Gabe, I didn't know about any of this, okay? I need a few minutes to digest all of this," I answered gently. "And you know nothing about me."

"It doesn't matter, I belong to you," he said, pulling off his shirt before he started working on his pants. "I'll do whatever, be whatever you need me to be so that you're always happy."

My jaw just about hit the ground at his words. What did you say to that? And as I watched the beautiful man in front of me continue to remove his clothes, I didn't want to say anything that would stop him. And didn't that just make me a son of a bitch?

CHAPTER 3

"Gabe, please, I need you to stop," I whispered, moments later when he started undressing me. I was drooling as I watched his lithe body move, but I knew there would be no going back if I didn't stop this now. "Please, baby. I need you to get dressed so I can show you a few things before there's no going back."

"As you wish," he replied, looking completely crushed. Quickly, I pulled him into my arms and mashed my mouth down on his. He moaned beautifully and parted his lips for me. I swiped my tongue around the inside of his mouth before pulling back.

"It's not that I don't want you, baby," I whispered against his lips. "I want you to know fully what you're getting into. Just because the sisters and Alejandro say that you belong to me, doesn't mean you don't have a say in it. If we do this, I want it to be because you want to be with me. Not because you think you have to."

"I do want you," Gabe said, smiling at me as he pulled his jeans back on. I was sad to see him cover up again. For one so short, he had a huge cock. And he was completely hairless, which I'd always found to be a turn-on.

"There are things about me you need to know, Gabe," I explained as he pulled his shirt back on. "I feed off others' lust, which means I have to be involved in the activities."

"I like the idea of watching you with someone," Gabe purred, rubbing on me as if a cat.

"You do, do you?" I asked harshly. "Fine, we'll see if this is what you really want."

I grabbed his hand and pulled him with me out of the office. Opening the door to Mick's office, I saw he was bent over the couch being fucked by Alex.

"Mick, I need a favor. Can I borrow Alex?" I asked, dropping Gabe's hand.

"No, but you can join in." Mick panted, holding out some lube to me. "Would you like Cal to fuck you, baby?"

"Very much if it would please you, my one and only." Alex grunted as he thrust into Mick's hole. I rolled my eyes as I made my way to them. Taking the bottle of lube from Mick, I moved around them so I was behind Alex.

"I like him to wear a plug always." Mick snickered, seeing the shock on my face when I saw the large butt plug in his ass. "It keeps him constantly frisky."

"I'll bet," I answered, unzipping my fly and shoving my pants and boxer briefs down to my knees. I squirted some lube on my cock and rubbed it in before pulling out the plug. Lining my dick up, I pushed forward; Alex's body opened up nicely and just about sucked me in. I started a hard and fast pace, drinking in Alex's lust as I pounded into his ass.

Hearing a gasp from the doorway, I saw Gabe's mouth hanging open as he watched us.

"This is what I do to feed." I grunted as I fucked Alex's ass raw. "I fuck and let others suck me off, feeding on their lust, Gabe. Is this what you want? A mate who will turn to others for what he needs?"

I knew I was being a complete bastard, but I figured brutal honesty was the only way to get through to Gabe what I really was. He smiled widely at me as he walked towards us. Gabe reached out and touched my ass with his hands. The surge of power I felt had me shooting my load into Alex instantly. Alex and Mick had the same reaction, crying out loudly as they came.

When I was spent, I slumped down to my knees as Alex collapsed on top of Mick.

"That was fantastic! Can I try your fae?" Mick gasped, trying to catch his breath.

"No fucking way," I growled, turning to Gabe. "You might like sharing me, but I don't share."

"It's not really sharing if I'm involved," Gabe answered as he knelt down in front of me. "I don't like the idea of you sneaking off and fucking someone behind my back, Cal. But I loved watching you take him, knowing I could touch you and join in."

"Really?" I asked at the same time as Mick. Gabe nodded as he took my hand and moved it to the fly of his jeans. I felt his cock was so hard it was about to break the fabric. "So as long as I don't do this without you, you're okay with it?"

"Very alright with it; it turns me on." Gabe purred, licking the side of my neck.

"You really are the dirtiest virgin I've ever met," Mick said, raising his head up to look at us. "And how did you get us to come like that? Alex doesn't climax unless ordered and lust demons can't come until after our partners do."

"I don't know. Did I mess up your feeding?" Gabe asked, his bottom lip sticking out in the sexiest pout I'd ever seen.

"Not for me, that was awesome!" Mick exclaimed as he and Alex got up. "I still feel the power racing through me."

"I do too," I said, realizing it might have been the best feeding I'd ever had. "Alex, are you okay?"

"I'm completely spent, but no more than as if I'd made love to my one and only for hours," Alex answered with a shrug. "I'm a shifter though, we recover quickly."

"Which is why you're the perfect baby for me,"
Mick said, wrapping himself around Alex when the man sat
down. "No more trial period, Alex. I want you to move in
with me and be only mine."

"Really, my love?" Alex exclaimed, wrapping his
arms around Mick. "You make me so happy, my one and
only."

With a wave of my hand, I tucked my cock back
into my pants and zipped up. I took Gabe's hand and
quietly led us from the room, closing the door behind us.

"I think they need some alone time, Gabe," I said as
I walked to the elevators. "I want to show you my place."

"Will you make love to me there?" Gabe asked, his
face brightening. I waited until we were in the elevator, key
card swiped, and the button to my floor pushed before
answering. Each of us had a floor to ourselves, and several
floors above that were the smaller apartments for
employees and pretty much all the wrath demons we
worked with. The five of us designed how we wanted our
own floors. I was on the sixth floor of our fifteen floor
building.

"This is really what you want? To be mated to a lust
demon and have our children?" I asked, eyeing him
carefully.

"Not just any lust demon, Cal. I want to be mated to

you," he answered, staring at me intently. He leapt into my arms when I opened them, wrapping himself around me. I had to admit, he felt so perfect in my arms, as if he was meant to be held by me. "I want to make you happy. The idea of having kids is a little weird to me, but the more I learn about you the more I like the idea. Can you imagine it? Having a little Cal running around that's ours?"

I thought about it for a few moments. The elevator opened, and I walked us off of it. I really did love the idea of our child growing inside of Gabe. "Yes, baby. I really like the idea. If we do this, I promise to always protect you and put you first."

"And I promise to always be there for you and make you happy," Gabe replied, kissing my neck. "Please, Cal, make love to me?"

"How can I refuse such an offer?" I moaned, rubbing my hands over his tight little ass as we made our way to my bedroom.

"Hopefully you can't." Gabe giggled. I loved the sound of his giggle; it made me hard as a rock knowing it was just for me.

"I don't want to." I moaned as he latched onto my ear. With a wave of my hand, we were naked as I tossed him down onto the bed.

"That's a really neat trick." He panted as he eyed my

body. "You're so hot, Cal. I want to touch you, but it's like I don't know where to start."

"Wherever you want, baby, I'm all yours now," I answered, climbing onto the bed. "I might need to feed with others, but I'm only yours now, Gabe."

"And I'm yours," he said, smiling up at me as I positioned my body over him. "I love how you surround me; it makes me feel safe and desired."

"Oh, you're desired, my sprite." I purred, leaning down to lick his lips. Gabe moaned, opening his mouth to me, and I took full advantage. I thrust my tongue inside, exploring my hot little fae. He surprised me by sucking on my tongue, and it just about unglued me. As I ran my hands over his body, he was so fucking responsive I knew I was a goner.

"How are we going to get this to fit in my ass?" Gabe asked as his fingers softly touched my cock.

"With lots of prep and fun," I answered, licking the side of his neck. He squirmed and gasped at my attention, making me feel about ten feet tall. I kept doing it while reaching over for the lube on the night stand. When I had it, I started licking my way down his tight, lithe body. I paid special attention to his nipples when I found out they were such a hot spot for him. Gabe went wild when I took one into my mouth and bit gently.

"Please, Cal, I feel like I'm going to burn up." Gabe whimpered.

"Okay, sweetheart." I chuckled, loving how eager he was for me. I swirled my tongue in his belly button as I moved down him. When I got to the large cock bobbing in my face, I knew I had to taste him. I couldn't get over that such a small man had this wide eight inch cock between his legs. Licking the slit, I moaned at the taste of his pre-cum. It was an ambrosia of sweet fruits.

I squirted some lube on my fingers, smiling up at him as I spread his legs wider for me. Gabe gave me a nod that he was ready, and I rubbed my fingers over his tight hole as I sucked the head of his cock into my mouth. Just as I pushed a single finger into him, Gabe screamed loudly, his dick exploding in my mouth. I watched the bliss on his face as I swallowed down everything he had to give me.

"I'm so sorry," he whispered, pulling away from me.

"For what?" I asked, completely confused as he made his way to the headboard and curled into a ball.

"I came already," he answered, not looking at me. "I couldn't help it. How am I to please you if I can't even hold off until the sex?"

"Listen to me, Gabe," I growled as I reached for him. His eyes went wide as I grabbed his leg and slid him across the sheets until he was back under me. I leaned down so we were nose to nose. "I love that I gave you that pleasure. It's hot the way you respond to my touch and want me so badly you're begging for me. You taste like heaven, and I plan on making you come like that as often as I can."

"Really?" Gabe gasped.

"Oh yeah, it was fucking hot." I purred as I licked his lips. "Don't ever hold your desire back from me, Gabe."

"So you're not mad?"

"Not in the slightest," I answered as I moved between his legs again. I sat back on my heels as he smiled and spread his legs widely for me. Looking at his tight, pink hole that seemed to quiver at just my stare, I got hard enough to pound steel nails. I ran my fingers over him before pushing in a finger again. Gabe cried out, moving his hips as he planted his feet on the bed. Glancing up, I saw the pleasure and lust he felt for me on his face. "Pinch your perfect nipples for me, baby."

Gabe's eyes went wide, his mouth partially open as he nodded and ran his hands over his chest. I slipped in a second finger as he pinched himself. Scissoring them around, I watched my baby as he moaned and writhed on my bed. I growled my approval as I stretched him out as fast as I could without hurting him. Moments later, he was ready for more, and I slid a third finger inside of his tight ass.

"I feel so full, Cal," he moaned, pushing his hips down on my fingers. "I want more."

"Just a little more, baby. I don't want to hurt you."

"You would never hurt me, I know that," he answered. Glancing up at him, I saw the trust and innocence on his face.

"Gabe, how old are you, sweetheart?"

"I just turned twenty-one a few days ago," he replied, his eyebrows scrunching together. "Does it really matter?"

"It does to me because I plan on corrupting you." I chuckled as I pushed in a fourth finger. When it went in easily, I was convinced he was ready for me. Gabe whimpered when I pulled my fingers out, using the lube still on them to slick up my cock. I leaned forward, lining up my dick with his tight hole and started to work it into him.

"Oh fuck." He screamed as I pushed past the first ring in his ass.

"Are you okay, Gabe?" I asked, freezing where I was, worried I'd hurt him.

"Yes, it burns a bit." Gabe hissed, his dick getting hard again. "Don't stop, Cal. I want all of you."

"You have all of me, my sprite," I answered as I

gently pushed inside of him farther. As I moved in and out of him, I was able to work more of my cock into him each time. We both moaned loudly as I finally bottomed out. Leaning over, I kissed him deeply as I moved my arms under his shoulders. Gabe responded by wrapping his arms and legs around me. I swear there wasn't a centimeter of space between our bodies.

I pulled out slowly as we kept kissing before thrusting back into him gently. It was then I was hit with the fact that this was the first time I'd ever made love. It wasn't the slow pace, but the concern I felt that I please Gabe more than receive my own pleasure.

"You're all mine now, Gabe. Forever mine, baby," I whispered in his ear as his short nails dug into my back. "I will protect you always, kill anyone who tries to take you from me."

"Yes." He hissed as he bit the side of my neck gently. I moved off of him a little so I could look down at him.

"I'm not kidding, Gabe. Now that I've had you, no one else," I said as I kept thrusting into him. "Say it, Gabe. Swear it to me that you'll always be only mine."

"I swear that I am now, and forever, only yours, Cal." He panted as I picked up the pace. His words spurring me on as nothing ever had. "I am yours as you are mine. No one else may ever have me."

"All mine," I growled, kissing him fiercely. I changed my angle, making sure to hit his sweet spot with each thrust.

"What the fuck is that?" He gasped, fisting the sheets in his hands.

"That would be your prostate, Gabe." I chuckled as he nodded, mouth parted as he moaned. "Touch yourself, baby. I want to see you stroke that gorgeous cock while I take you."

"Yes," he hissed as he moved his hand down to his dick. I watched as ran his index finger over the slit, my nostrils flaring when I saw the pre-cum leaking out. He stroked it a few times before tensing up and screaming my name as he climaxed. The muscles in his ass squeezed my cock as I kept pushing into him.

"Gabe," I cried out as my orgasm swept over me. As soon as the first spurt of cum shot inside of him, I felt more than my own climax. I closed my eyes, realizing it was Gabe's emotions. The desire in him to be loved and cherished was so deep and ingrained in him, it almost brought tears to my eyes. I could see how, even though the sisters were good to him, he'd always wanted a family of his own.

"Is that really how you feel?" Gabe asked softly,

snapping me out of his head and staring down at him.

"About what, baby?" I answered, my eyebrows scrunching together.

"That you're evil because you're a demon and don't deserve love," he whispered, his eyes filling up with tears. "I saw inside of you, Cal. You're not evil at all. How many couples have you helped find each other over the centuries so they could have the happiness you didn't think you could ever have?"

"Lots," I replied quietly, almost grateful he could see my fears without me ever having to say them.

"Come here, my mate," Gabe said, smiling up at me as he held out his arms. I leaned over and kissed him as I wrapped my body around him. He did the same, though I was careful not to crush him with my weight. "That was everything I'd ever hoped for and more, Cal."

"Me too, baby. Me too," I replied, turning so we were on our sides. It was the first time I'd ever held anyone or snuggled after sex. Hell, it was the first time I'd ever even wanted to. I needed to get Gabe into a hot bath though; it would help his soreness after his first time.

"Don't leave me yet," Gabe said, looking up at me as I moved off the bed.

"I'm not leaving you, baby." I chuckled as I pulled him up into my arms. "We're going to take a nice bubble bath so you won't be too sore tomorrow."

"When can we do that again?" Gabe giggled. I smiled down at him, watching him wiggle his eyebrows at me as I walked us into the adjoining bathroom. With a wave of my hand, the large tub was full with warm water and bubbles. "I really like that trick."

"It comes in handy," I agreed as I stepped into the tub. Sitting down, I positioned Gabe in between my legs as I reached over for a washcloth. I dunked it under the water, then started running it all over his body, loving the feel of him in my arms. Gabe opened up for me, moaning as he threw his legs over mine. I kissed his neck and shoulders as I washed his chest and stomach. "Baby, you keep this up and we're going to have sex again *real* soon."

"Okay," Gabe said, getting to his feet and bending over to rest his hands on the side of the tub. He wiggled his ass at me, giving me a fantastic view of his hole, already stretched from our earlier lovemaking. "Fuck me raw, Cal."

"You're going to be sore as is, baby." I chuckled, moving over behind him. Grabbing the cheeks of his ass, I licked his sweet hole a few times.

"Oh fuck, oh fuck." Gabe whimpered as I teased him. Reaching between his legs, I stroked him as I licked his puckered hole. Gabe was screaming and coming in no time.

"Is sprite the same as nympho?" I asked as Gabe sagged back into my arms.

"I don't think so." Gabe panted as he snuggled against me under the bubbles. "It's like ever since I turned twenty-one I've had a hard-on I just can't get rid of. Seeing how hot you are and that you're mine now hasn't helped it."

"I'll try to be less sexy, sweetheart." I laughed, taking the washcloth again and cleaning him up. After a few minutes, I realized Gabe was asleep. Smiling as I cleaned him, I took my sweet time memorizing every inch of the man I was already falling for. I just hoped I was enough to make him happy.

CHAPTER 4

I was sitting at the main bar the next day hours before opening, reading the sprite handbook, as Alejandro called it. I had so many questions after the short time I'd spent with Gabe I knew I'd needed help. Alejandro had only just dropped it off, saying to inform him as soon as Gabe was showing signs of being pregnant. That was still something I'd have to come to terms with.

"You fucking bastard," Mike screamed as he stormed towards me. I'd barely turned to face him when I got a face full of fist.

"What did I do?" I asked, backing away from him as I held my chin. If I'd been human he'd have broken it with that shot. Beck came racing over to us, laying a hand on Mike's shoulder and drank down all his anger. When he was done, Mike was kneeling on the floor in front of me, looking completely defeated. "Mike, what's wrong?"

"You set me up with Noah, but he's taken," he answered quietly. The despair I felt in him almost took away my ability to breathe. "I went to pick him up for our date, and some guy answered the door saying Noah was his. I don't get it; the guy was hideous, scars all over his face and mean as can be. Why would Noah want to be with him?"

"He wouldn't," I said, waving Beck back over. "A halfer got to the twink I was with the other night. You said his name is Noah?"

"You didn't even know his name?" Mike replied, looking up with me at disgust.

"Mike, it's a sex club; we don't always get names," I said gently. "But I know Noah is single and really into you. I don't think he's being kept from you because it's what he wants."

"T-that guy's hurting him?" Mike stuttered, looking even more forlorn.

"What's going on?" Gabe asked as he ran off the elevator towards me. "I felt your distress."

"One of the men I've been with has been taken by a halfer," I explained. I had already explained to Gabe what they were and why they followed us around last night. "Mike, come with us, I need you to show us where Noah lives."

"I thought that guy was off. Why didn't I do something?" he asked, standing and walking with us to the main entrance. I was glad I still had the handbook from Alejandro.

"There was nothing you could do, Mike," I answered gently as I handed Gabe the book. "See if there's anything in there about how you can kill halfers."

"I'm on it," Gabe replied as he climbed into one of the SUVs. Once everyone was in, I hopped in as well, closing the door behind us.

"Mike, there's a lot you're not going to understand right now," I told him as I took his hands. "We'll get Noah back, that's all you need to know. The rest, I'll explain later."

"Okay," he said quietly, then gave directions to Noah's apartment to Beck. The drive over wasn't far but seemed to drag on, as everyone was lost in their own thoughts. Finally, the car stopped and we all got out, following Mike's lead. I cringed when I saw the shit hole apartments Noah lived in. That would be something else I'd be taking care of after we got Noah back.

"Stay behind us," I told Mike and Gabe as we got to Noah's door.

"Wait, I know what I need to do," Gabe said, moving next to me.

"If you can do it, but don't put yourself in harm's way," I replied, letting my voice show that I wasn't fucking around. He gave me a quick nod before Beck kicked in the door. I followed him in, a few more wrath demons behind me before Gabe and Mike.

"He's mine," the halfer hissed as we came into the bedroom. There was another one with his cock buried in

Noah, who was screaming for help.

"No he's not," I growled, about to light him up. Before I could, there was a blinding light that filled the room. Even I had to cover my eyes for a few moments. When it was gone, so were the halfers. Gabe was slumped on the floor, but awake. I moved to him as Mike sprinted for Noah. "Baby, are you okay?"

"Tired and hungry," Gabe answered as I lifted him into my arms. "But that was wicked cool."

"You find new and inventive ways to amaze me, sweetheart," I said, shaking my head as I held him close.

"Mike? Is that really you, Mike?" Noah cried out as Mike and Beck untied him. Mike whipped off Noah's blindfold and gently pulled the smaller man into his arms.

"Yeah, it's me, Noah," he whispered as Noah sobbed in his arms. "It's okay now, Noah. You're safe."

"You won't want me now," Noah whimpered, trying to get away from Mike. "Not after what they did to me."

"That wasn't your fault, Noah. I still want you, baby," Mike answered, peppering kisses over Noah's face. "I'm never going to let you go, Noah."

"Beck, get one of your guys to pack some things for Noah," I ordered, wanting us to get out of there in case more halfers came. "Also call our doctor and tell him to meet us at the club. Mike, Noah, we need to leave in case more come."

"I'm right behind you," Mike replied, grabbing a throw blanket and covering up Noah. I carried Gabe out of the dilapidated apartment, Mike followed with Noah in his arms. We made our way downstairs and into the SUVs.

"Take us back, Beck, and the rest will take the other car," I told the driver. I looked down at Gabe who was smiling widely up at me. "What's that smile for?"

"I saved him. I killed the halfers and saved Noah," he said, still smiling. "Sorry, maybe it's not the time to be smiling, but I'm just really proud of myself."

"I'm proud of you too, baby," I replied, giving him a quick kiss. "What are you in the mood to eat?"

"Can we have whatever we want?" Noah asked from next to me, nestled in Mike's arms.

"You, my dear, can have anything and everything you want," I answered, feeling incredible guilt for what had happened to him. "I've got a lot of explaining to do."

"I figured you were very different," Noah said quietly. "I'd like Jimmy John's please. That's what my gram used to get me when I was sad."

"Of course," I replied, getting out when the vehicle stopped. The night I'd met Mike and Noah, I read Noah's mind and saw he was suffering from a recent loss. Now that he was thinking about it, I got the whole story. Looking down at Gabe, I could see he did too. Noah's grandma had recently passed and was the only family he'd ever had.

When I saw the doctor we called on from time to time, I gave him a nod to join us. We all got on the elevator; Gabe waved my keycard and pushed the button for our floor. After the doors opened, we all walked into our apartment.

"Mike, there's a guest room down the hall on your left with a private bath," I said as I walked towards the living room. "Doc, you're with them. Noah's been abused."

"I understand," he answered and followed behind Mike.

"It's not your fault, Cal," Gabe said softly, running his hands over my shoulders as I sat us down.

"Yes, it is," I replied, pulling out my phone. I dialed the number for information, who connected me with the local Jimmy John's. Gabe giggled softly as I ordered enough party platters, chips, cookies, and pickles for a small army. I gave the guy my credit card number, saying to include a five hundred dollar tip if they could bring some of the order right away and get the rest when it was ready.

"I'm not sure I'm *that* hungry, Cal." Gabe laughed when I got off the phone.

"Well then, we have dinner for the staff of the club too," I answered with a shrug. I sent Eaton a text to get everyone to my apartment right away. Just then the elevator doors opened and Beck came into the apartment with a few of his men. My apartment was huge, each of us having a full floor to ourselves. "Tell your guys at the door I ordered a ton of food and to bring it right up."

Beck talked into his radio as I held onto Gabe, feeling as if he was the only thing that could keep me grounded. I was in a daze as everything and everyone moved around me, thinking over and over again that this was all my fault. Noah was raped and suffered because I'd played with him the other night.

I listened as the doctor filled in Mike and Eaton on what Noah needed, that there was no permanent damage physically. But Noah's main issue was that he was afraid to be alone and worried Mike wouldn't want him now that he was damaged.

After that, Gabe and Beck filled everyone in on what happened. The food came, and I watched as everyone ate. Mike and Noah came out of the spare bedroom, Mike carrying him since Noah's legs had been badly beaten.

"Can you explain what's going on, and why Noah?" Gabe asked Eaton on the side when Eaton went to come into the living room. "It's really been hard on Cal."

"Yeah, I got this, you just take care of my boy," Eaton replied, giving Gabe a wink.

"Always," Gabe said, giving me a kiss on my temple. Eaton sat down and started to explain to Mike and Noah what we were. Then what halfers were and why they went after Noah.

"This is because of you?" Noah gasped, shooting daggers at me with his stare. "How could you do this to me?"

"Don't," I said to Beck when he went over to take away their anger. "They deserve their rage towards me."

"I don't agree with that," Gabe replied, standing up. "This was not Cal's fault! I'm sorry that this happened and it sucks, but I won't let him take the blame for what those assholes did to you."

"Gabe, please," I said quietly, taking his hand.

"You didn't even warn us that we could be a target." Mike growled from his seat with Noah on his lap. "What if I'd not gone to see Noah and then came to yell at you?"

"I know and I'm sorry," I answered, standing and dropping Gabe's hand. "I know that's not enough, but I am very sorry. If I could have traded places with Noah, I would have."

Everyone just started at me until I couldn't take it anymore. I walked out of the living room and went to my bedroom, closing the door behind me. The living room exploded with shouting voices as I waved my clothes away and crawled into bed. I couldn't think of another time in my life when I'd ever felt so alone and depressed. The guilt I felt was overwhelming, and I knew it wanted to consume me.

"Cal, can I come in?" Gabe asked, opening the door and sticking his head in.

"No, I want to be alone please," I answered. Either Gabe came in and made me feel better, or he joined me in my dark place. Right then, I didn't want either one.

"Okay, my love," he said quietly and closed the door. I knew it had probably hurt him that I turned him away, and I appreciated him not pushing, but I just needed to deal alone right then. It wasn't that I didn't want to share my grief and pain with Gabe; I didn't know how to. And wasn't that what being in a relationship was all about? Being able to share the good and the bad?

It made me rethink the idea that my feeding off lust was going to be the hardest thing for Gabe to deal with. I'd been alone for centuries, closed off from others because I'd only ever had myself to rely on. Now that had changed, but what was the old addatage about teaching old dogs new tricks? And Gabe deserved everything, better than I could probably ever give him.

CHAPTER 5

A few days later, I was still in bed consumed with my guilt and grief. Added to what happened to Noah was the guilt for the way I was treating Gabe. Every time he crawled into bed, I turned away from him. We hadn't even spoken since he originally stuck his head in, or touched, nor had we done anything together. The darkness that had enveloped me was ruining our post-mating honeymoon phase.

The worst part was that I saw it happening and felt powerless to stop it. This wasn't something I could just smile my way through and pretend everything was alright. Because it wasn't. Because of me someone was raped and tortured. How did you move on from that?

I heard the door opening and closed my eyes, pretending I was asleep. I just wasn't ready to face anyone yet after what I'd done. Soft lips pressed against mine, and I opened my eyes, but it wasn't Gabe.

"Noah?" I asked softly, completely confused. He smiled at me as I sat up against the headboard.

"It wasn't your fault, Cal," he said, taking my hand. "I'm sorry I ever said that to you. I was angry and upset, but when I calmed down, I realized it wasn't your fault. You came to save me, Cal. You aren't the bad guy here."

"If you hadn't been with me—" I started to reply, but Noah put his hand over my mouth.

"Then I would never have found Mike," Noah said with a smile. "But what happened with the halfers wasn't your fault. You didn't know they would come after me. Eaton and your friends told me you increased security. Everyone thought since I'd left with Mike I'd be fine. This wasn't any one person's fault except the bastards Gabe killed."

"I'm so sorry." I whispered, tears filling up my eyes. "I didn't know, Noah. I really like you and Mike; I didn't mean for this to happen."

"I know that, and I'm not angry with you, Cal." He nodded. "Now you just have to stop being angry with yourself. I'm going to be okay. Mike still wants me, and the doctor is going to refer me to someone I can talk with. Soon I'll go back to work and move forward. You have a man who loves you and is scared shitless because he can't help you. Gabe's a mess, Cal."

"I don't know how to let him in," I answered, squeezing Noah's hand.

"Get your ass out of bed and talk with him. That's a good start," Noah replied, tugging at my hand. "Go be with your man and show Gabe you need him."

"Thank you, Noah," I said as we walked out of the

bedroom.

"Thank you for coming to save me," he replied, giving my cheek a quick kiss before pushing me towards the kitchen. I realized I was still naked and quickly waved my hand to put on some pajama pants. Nice of Noah to let me know he was getting a full view of my assets. I shook my head as I walked to the kitchen, and what I saw stopped me in my tracks.

Gabe was sitting on a stool at the counter, bent over his arms, sobbing. I raced to him and immediately picked him up in my arms.

"Baby, why are you crying? Are you hurt?" I asked, checking him over for wounds or marks.

"Do you forgive me, Cal?" he answered, wiping away tears as he stared up at me. "I'm sorry I got involved in the conversation, but I didn't feel like they should yell at you."

"Oh, Gabe," I whispered, my heart twisting in my chest at the realization that he thought I was mad at him this whole time. "I was never upset with you, sweetheart."

"Then why? Why are you pushing me away and not letting me in?" he cried as he threw his arms around my neck. "I didn't know what to do, I tried being there for you, but you don't want me. Should I just go?"

"No!" I gasped, hugging him tighter to me. "God,

Gabe, you didn't do anything wrong. I didn't know how to let you in, baby. I'm so sorry; I didn't know you thought I was upset with you. Please don't leave me, Gabe."

"I'm not going anywhere as long as you want me, Cal," he answered, peppering my face with kisses. "It was killing me not knowing how to help you."

"Gabe, I'm so sorry," I said, finally feeling the tears I'd not shed since I saw Noah in pain. "I didn't mean to shut you out, I just didn't know how to let you in, baby."

"Do you not want me, Cal? Is that why you wouldn't let me be there for you?"

"I want you, Gabe. I just don't know if I'm enough to make you happy," I answered honestly before I realized what I'd said. Carrying him in my arms like the precious cargo he was, I went back into our room, closing the door behind us. Laying him gently on the bed, I snuggled against him. "I've been alone for centuries, Gabe. I don't know how to be with someone else or have a real relationship."

"I don't know either, Cal," Gabe said gently. "But we have to do this together, shutting me out won't help us as a couple. Your pain is my pain. I just didn't know what that pain was exactly."

"I'm so sorry, baby," I replied before kissing him. Gabe moaned and wrapped his body around me. "Please forgive me, Gabe. I need you, I need you so fucking much it hurts. I'll try to let you in, I swear."

"I need you too, Cal." He gasped as I sucked on his earlobe. "You can't shut me out like that again, Cal. I didn't know what to do and I thought you didn't want me anymore."

"Never again, sweetheart," I said, licking along his collarbone. I waved away our clothes and some lube appeared in my hand. "I always want you, Gabe. I didn't feel I was worthy of you after everything that happened."

"That's not your choice to make." Gabe growled, taking my head in his hands. "That's *my* choice and I *choose* you, Cal. Don't ever decide things like that for me. We're partners, and if you want this to work, we have to make decisions together."

"I promise," I whispered, tears of relief escaping my eyes. Gabe's face softened as he kissed my cheeks and brushed away my tears. "Do you forgive me, Gabe?"

"I was never mad, Cal," he said gently. "Just confused and a little hurt that you didn't turn to me. That's why I thought you were angry with me."

"No, baby, I'll never be angry with you," I replied, shocked when he started giggling.

"Oh, there will be times that you're mad at me," Gabe said with a smile. "And there are going to be times I'm pissed at you, but we have to talk to each other, or we'll never make it."

"I promise to do better. I can't say I won't do it again, because I might, and I never want to lie to you, Gabe. But you have to do something for me, okay?"

"Anything," he answered without a moment's hesitation. It was that trust and belief in me that had me falling so hard and fast for Gabe.

"Next time you think I might be mad at you, ask me," I said, staring into his eyes. "I know I wasn't in a position to be forthcoming, but if I'd known you were upset and thought I was pissed at you, I would have."

"Deal." Gabe smiled up at me. I wrapped my arms around him, hugging him to me fiercely as he did the same. "I want you, Cal. I need to feel my mate and make love to him, but you stink."

"You sweet talker." I laughed as I picked him up and got off the bed. Gabe giggled and rubbed his erection against my stomach as I walked us into the shower stall. I preferred a separate shower from the bathtub; it gave me a chance to trick both of them out. "Warm, all three jets."

"That's so cool," Gabe said as the shower heads turned on to the perfect warm temperature. Then my mouth was on his, demanding and needy. He moaned and opened up for me perfectly.

"Can you wash us while I stretch you out?" I asked,

not wanting to stop, but remembering I smelled and hence the shower.

"I wanted to ask you about that," Gabe replied softly, turning the hottest shade of pink.

"You can ask me anything, Gabe," I said gently, realizing whatever it was, he was nervous.

"Can I take you?" he mumbled, burying his head in my neck. It took me a few seconds to realize what he was taking about. Then it hit me, Gabe wanted to be on the giving end.

"I've never done that," I answered honestly. He nodded against my neck, not responding with words. "But I'd be willing to try it with you, my mate."

"Really?" he asked, his head popping up to look at me with big eyes. "You'd let me try?"

"Sure." I chuckled, rubbing my fingers over the crease of his ass. "I tend to be the aggressor and top, but that doesn't mean I'm not willing to try new things. If you really want to fuck me, I think it's hot. I reserve the right to not like it though."

"I love you, Cal," Gabe said, causing me to almost drop him. I stared at him for several long moments before he started to squirm in my arms. "I'm sorry, I shouldn't have said that already. Forget it."

"Gabe, wait," I replied, feeling like a heel when I

saw how hurt and dejected he looked. I held him to me so he couldn't slide down me. "I'm falling for you, Gabe. I know that, but I've seen a lot over the centuries and a lot of people use the word love when they mean lust. I want to be sure of the difference before I ever tell someone I love them, okay? It's not that I don't care for you deeply, because I do."

"But you're not there yet." He nodded, giving me a half smile. "I've never felt about anyone the way I feel for you, Cal."

"I feel the same way, baby," I said carefully. "I just want to be absolutely sure before I use those words. Please don't be mad or upset."

"I'm not," he replied, taking the lube from me. "Now get clean as I get your hot ass ready."

"My dirty little sprite," I purred as I let him slowly slide down my body to his feet. "Just remember, I might not be able to say the words yet, but you're the first person I've ever trusted to fuck me."

"That's a good start." Gabe giggled as he moved my hips to turn around and face the shower wall. I reached for the ledge, picking up the bar of soap before starting to quickly rub it all over my body.

Glancing over my shoulder, I saw and felt Gabe run his slicked fingers over my hole. He smiled at me as he pushed one in. I moaned loudly, feeling my knees weaken. Even though his fingers were smaller than mine, it was the first time anyone had ever played with my ass.

"My big lust demon likes that, huh?"

"Yes," I hissed, pushing back on his finger. "I need more, baby."

"Only if you keep washing," Gabe said, giving my ass a smack. That was enough motivation for me. I soaped up and rinsed off before he slipped in another finger. Reaching for the shampoo, I squirted some into my hand, then put it back on the shelf.

"Fuck, that's good, baby." I groaned when he pushed in a third finger and started wiggling them around. I forgot about my hair until I got another slap on my ass. Looking over at Gabe, he gestured with his free hand to my head. Chuckling, I lathered up my hair and rinsed. "Okay, I'm clean, no more teasing."

"Fair enough," Gabe replied as he pulled his fingers from my ass. I braced my hands against the wall as I bent over, offering myself up to him. Gabe lined up his cock and slowly pushed into me.

"Holy shit!" I gasped, leaning over farther.

"Did I hurt you, Cal?" Gabe asked, concern in his voice.

"It burns a little." I panted, trying to deal with the

onslaught of sensations. "More shocked at how good this feels. I see why people like it."

"Just wait, it gets better." He purred, pushing in farther. And god, was my little sprite right. I had stars bursting behind my eyes as the line between pleasure and pain got mixed up. We both moaned when he finally bottomed out inside of me, our balls brushing against each other. "Tell me when you're ready for me to move."

"Move! Fuck, don't wait," I said, pushing back against him.

"You're really tight, Cal. I won't last long," he replied as he slowly pulled back out. Gabe thrust hard into me, causing me to cry out in pleasure.

"Oh, harder, baby. Give it to me harder." I groaned, trying to not simply bend in half so he'd go deeper. Then I thought, *fuck it*. I walked my hands down the wall until they touched the floor, loving how the angle was changing.

"So fucking hot. I didn't know you were so flexible." Gabe grunted as he pounded into my ass.

"Neither did I," I said honestly. It seemed he was bringing out all types of new things in me. "Fill up my ass, sweetheart."

"Yes," he hissed loudly as I felt him stiffen up before crying out my name as his climax overtook him. I tightened the muscles in my ass, milking his cock as I tried to keep his orgasm going. When he was finally spent, he collapsed over me. "That was awesome!"

"Um, Gabe, I didn't, ya know, finish?" I asked, not really wanting to ruin his post-orgasmic glow, but I was dying to come.

"I stretched myself out while stretching you." He panted as he stood where he was. "I don't think I'm able to move just right now though."

I chuckled as I reached back and held him to me before turning around to face him. He had the most adorable smirk on his face as I lifted him into my arms. I wrapped his arms and legs around me before slowly lowering him onto my throbbing cock.

"Oh shit, I'm going to come again." He groaned as I pushed his back against the wall of the shower.

"My baby's a nympho, not a sprite." I grunted as I pounded into his tight, but stretched, hole. It hit me as I took him, he'd thought enough of my pleasure to stretch himself in case I didn't like being on the receiving end. Damn. He really was the perfect man. But something inside of me was screaming not to tell him that I loved him yet. Fear?

Pushing the thoughts aside, I focused on the hot man in my arms. I kissed him deeply, thrusting my tongue into his mouth as I did my cock into his ass. Breaking the kiss, I stared into his deep lavender eyes. The intensity of the feelings I saw in his eyes, and the ones I felt, pushed me over the edge. I screamed as came harder than I could ever remember, never looking away from his stare.

"Cal," he cried out, filling the space between us with his orgasm. I mashed my mouth down on his, swallowing his cries of pleasure as I felt them seep into my soul. I might not be sure if I loved Gabe yet, but he was everything to me.

"Now that my body is spent, can we eat? I'm starving," I said when we finally regulated our heart rates.

"Me too." Gabe purred, licking my neck.

"Seriously, I'm just going to call you nympho from now on." I chuckled as my spent cock slipped out of him. He giggled as I lowered him to his feet, and we both quickly cleaned up. After we stepped out of the shower, and dried off, I had an idea. I took his hand and led him to the bed where I gently pushed him onto his stomach.

"Cal?" Gabe asked, glancing at me over his shoulder as I dug through the nightstand. Finding what I wanted, I held up the large butt plug for him to see. "Cal, what's that?"

"It's a butt plug, baby. It will keep this sweet ass stretched for me so you can ride my cock whenever my little nympho wants to." I chuckled as I squirted some lube on it.

"And I'm the dirty one?" Gabe's giggle turned into a loud moan as I pushed in the plug.

"That's why you're so perfect for me," I answered as I rubbed his ass once it was in.

"How am I supposed to *not* be horny with this in?" he asked, standing up. Gabe gestured to his hard dick before we both burst out laughing.

"Later, I'm hungry," I said, waving pajama bottoms onto both of us. He was still laughing as I took his hand and led him out of the bedroom.

"Fine, but you're going to need to feed your lust soon, and I want to watch," Gabe replied as we walked into the kitchen. "I like the idea of someone giving you a blow job while you watch me play with myself. Maybe just wiggling this plug around might be enough for me to come."

"No wonder you needed a lust demon to be your mate." I chuckled as I pulled a couple of leftover sandwiches out of the fridge. Grabbing a couple bags of potato chips and pop, I joined Gabe at the counter.

"The book Alejandro gave us says I'm going to be like this whenever I'm not knocked up," Gabe replied in between bites. "It's still weird for me, you know? This idea of being pregnant."

"It is for me too and not just because you're a man,"
I answered thoughtfully after a few moments. "I never
thought I would have children; they don't normally mix in
with the idea of being a demon."

"But you want them, right?" Gabe asked quietly,
lowering his sandwich.

"With you? Yeah, I really do, baby," I replied,
smiling at him as I reached over and squeezed his hand.
"The idea of having little Gabe sprites running around
warms my heart."

"Good. Until then, we can just enjoy my never
ending need for sex." He giggled, giving me his brightest
smile. I groaned as I saw the tent in his pajama pants. I was
in for a really interesting life, and I knew I would love
every minute of it.

CHAPTER 6

Gabe and I had just finished my lust feeding later that day, as Gabe requested we do it, of course. We were riding back up in the elevator with Eaton, Mick, and Alex. They were filling me in on what I missed with the club during my meltdown. Gabe and I got off the elevator first and walked into the living room.

Noah stood quickly from where he was sitting next to Mike and went pale. And I'm not just talking he lost some color; it was like every ounce of blood left his body. I watched in horror as he stared past me and started shaking violently. Mike saw it too and tried getting his attention. I pulled Gabe behind me and pushed him towards the kitchen as I tried to figure out what was going on. I cringed when I saw Noah's pants get wet as he peed himself.

What the fuck was going on?

"How did you get free?" Alex gasped, drawing our attention. He realized he'd slipped up and went to bolt for the elevator. Eaton reached out and grabbed him by the throat, holding him in place.

"I thought you said they were all dead," Noah squeaked out from Mike's arms.

"Alex was one of the ones who took you, Noah?" I asked, completely shocked. Looking at Mick's forlorn face,

I knew he felt the same.

"Alex, explain yourself immediately," Mick ordered, turning towards the man with his hands on his hips.

"Oh go fuck yourself, you pathetic Dom wannabe," Alex growled at him. I felt the air vibrate around Alex.

"You shift and I'll snap your neck before you have the chance," Eaton snarled in his face. "Why, Alex? Why would you get involved with halfers?"

"Everyone has a price." Alex smirked then pointed at Mick. "Mine was a million to put up with his shit and tell them who you guys fucked from the club."

"I-I thought…" Mick stammered, looking like he'd been struck.

"Yeah right." Alex scoffed. "You're a hot piece of ass, but I wanted to vomit every time you ordered me around like some Dom poser."

"Enough," I shouted, not wanting to see Noah's or Mick's distress at the hands of this asshole. "Who else was taken?"

"Fuck you, I'm dead either way," Alex spat at me.

"Yes, but how you die is your choice," Eaton said, heating up his hand with the fire we could control. Alex let out a sharp cry as his neck started to burn. "We can make it quick or very, very long."

"In the warehouse district," Alex replied as he slumped to his knees. "The old seafood packing plant. They're holed up there with about five or so people they want to feed off of."

"Take Noah into the other room, Mike," Mick said calmly.

"Gabe, go with them and see that they have what they need," I told Gabe, giving him a knowing look. Mike lifted Noah into his arms and left with Gabe following him. I went over to Mick and put my hand on his shoulder. "You don't have to do this; we can take care of him."

"No. This is my fault, I let him into our lives," Mick replied. Eaton took a step back as Alex braced himself to attack. Mick was quicker, shooting fire out of his hands and engulfing Alex. The man gave one scream of pain before collapsing and dying. It wasn't just normal fire; we could control how hot the fire burned, as well. In seconds, Alex was nothing more than a pile of ash.

I eyed my friend with concern as I pulled out my phone and called Beck. "Close the club; give everyone a free voucher to come back. Explain there's been an emergency."

"What's up, Cal?" he asked on the other end of the line.

"Alex was a traitor; he was working with the

halfers. He gave us the location of others being held," I explained.

"Fucking bastard, I'll tear him—" Beck snarled into the phone, but I cut him off.

"Mick took care of him. Get everyone out and close the club. Then I want every available demon we can get up in my apartment. We don't know how many there will be, Beck."

"Understood, Cal," he replied before hanging up.

"What's the plan?" Mick asked me.

"Maybe you should sit this one out, Mick?" Eaton asked as he tried to hug our friend.

"No, I need to see this through," he answered, pushing Eaton away. "I'll have my nervous breakdown afterwards. Right now, we need to rescue those I put in harm's way."

"Get on the phone with the doc," I told Mick, deciding busy work would be best for him right then. "Tell him what's going on and we don't know how many injured we have coming in. We can set up the club as triage until we know what we're dealing with. Get whatever medical supplies we keep in the storage room at the club, blankets, anything you can think of down there."

"I'm on it," Mick replied with a nod, walking towards the elevator. Eaton and I exchanged a look, realizing this might be something Mick never recovered from. He truly had cared for Alex. In all the years I'd known him, he'd only let two of his men ever move in with him. The last one had been centuries ago, until he found Alex. And it wasn't just the betrayal, but the cruel words he spoke as he was staring down death.

As I went in search of Gabe, I wondered how much it had cost Mick to take Alex's life like that. Realizing I'd need to talk to everyone about giving Mick support and watching him, I knocked on the door to the spare bedroom.

"How's Noah?" I asked Gabe as he let me in.

"I assured him he was safe now, but I think he took several steps back in his recovery." Gabe sighed. "I can't believe Alex was a part of this. How's Mick?"

"I don't know," I answered softly. And that was the truth; I could only imagine what my friend of centuries was feeling right then. Deciding to shelf the issue for more pressing ones, I walked into the bathroom. Mike was in the tub with Noah, holding the smaller man to his chest as they took a soak. "Alex will never hurt you again, Noah."

"I feel so stupid," he said quietly, looking at me with tears in his eyes. "I never asked how many were in the room when you guys saved me. I assumed all three had been there."

"We should have asked you, baby," Mike replied,

kissing his temple. "I don't think any of us ever thought anyone would ever work with the halfers."

"How's Mick?" Noah asked, softening my heart for the small man even more. He was upset and freaked out, but still checking on someone else.

"I really don't know." I sighed, running my fingers through my hair. "He really cared for Alex and what he said to Mick… I just don't know, Noah."

"This wasn't his fault," Noah said, snuggling against Mike. "None of this was any of your faults."

"It's hard not to feel responsible, Noah," I replied gently. "I felt bad enough for being negligent towards the people we fed off of, but Mick let Alex into our lives. I don't think it's going to be as easy for him to forgive himself."

"Well, I don't blame him, and I appreciate all you guys have done," Noah said, giving me a weak smile.

"Tell Cal what you do, Noah?" Gabe asked from behind me, wrapping his arms around my waist.

"I'm a pediatric nurse," Noah answered, glancing between the two of us. "Why does that matter?"

"Because sprites are very special fae," I said, pulling Gabe around to the front of me. "They can have babies, and we plan on having lots of them."

"And I think a pediatric nurse would be a handy

person to have around," Gabe explained smiling up at me. "We could talk to Alejandro about getting Noah trained in how to take care of fae children."

"Smart and sexy," I said, giving him a quick kiss. "Would you be willing to leave the hospital and be employed by us, Noah? We could give you one of the smaller apartments upstairs as part of your salary."

"Well, I think Mike and I are going to move in together," Noah replied nervously, glancing from Mike to me. Mike smiled widely and nodded.

"That's the best part." Gabe giggled, getting a raised eyebrow from me. "Mike, tell Cal what you do."

"I'm a construction foreman," Mike replied, looking confused as the light bulb went off over my head.

"You've just thought of everything, haven't you, my little sprite?"

"It's why you keep me around," he answered, pursing his lips at me for a kiss. Chuckling, I bent down and gave him another one.

"Mind filling us in?" Mike asked, glancing between us.

"We're looking for a location to open another club," I answered. "Mick's got a few properties we've put bids on, but we need an architect and foreman to get the place built. Want a job?"

"I could stay here, with Noah?" he asked, smiling widely. I gave him a nod as he hugged Noah to him. "Then I gladly accept."

"Wonderful." Gabe clapped. "Noah?"

"I love working at the hospital, but I didn't make much. I mean, you saw where I was living," Noah answered, biting his lower lip. "I was saving for medical school too, so I didn't spend much of my salary."

"Even better! You could be a supernatural doctor, just think of how exclusive your clientele would be," Gabe said, completely excited, almost vibrating in my embrace. "He could go to school while he helps us with the babies, right, Cal?"

"Like I'm going to say no to you when you're giving me that adorable hopeful look." I chuckled as his lower lip came out. Leaning down, I nipped it quickly before turning back to Mike and Noah. "I'll need to check with the other guys, but I think it's a great idea. We've got a few two bedroom apartments upstairs since most of the staff likes to live on premises. You can check them out and pick whichever you like."

"Thanks, Cal," Noah said, smiling at me as Mike nodded in agreement.

"One other thing, now that I know what you do, Mike. Do you know how we can get blueprints for the old seafood packing plant?" I asked. "We're going in, but I prefer not going in blind."

"Yeah, I got a friend who can hook us up." He nodded.

"Sweet, thanks," I replied as I took Gabe's hand and left them alone. I waited until we were in the hallway before I lifted Gabe into my arms, leaned him against the wall, and kissed him. Putting every feeling I had for him into the kiss, I smiled as we parted, and I saw his face was flushed as he panted.

"What was that for?" he asked, raising an eyebrow.

"Two things. One, because I think what you just did for them was wonderful and selfless," I answered. "Two, I have a favor to ask you."

"Anything, Cal."

"Don't come with us to the warehouse," I said, knowing he wouldn't like it. "I was stupid for ever letting you come to the apartment with us, and we don't know how many are going to be at the plant. Please, Gabe, I don't want you hurt."

He eyed me over for a few moments, then tapped my arm for me to let him down. I lowered him to his feet, bracing for his reaction.

"Cal, I hear what you're saying," he finally replied, looking as if he was choosing his words carefully. "I won't go if that's what you really want, but I wish you wouldn't ask this of me. I feel the same way, but I'm not asking you to sit this one out. I was able to help the last time, and I could again."

"But we don't know what killing them does to you," I answered. I was shocked at how calm and logical he was being, though I kind of felt like an ass for expecting anything else. Gabe had shown me how smart and loving he was a few times already. "And there will be a lot more than two this time, Gabe."

"Okay, I can see that," Gabe replied, scrunching his eyebrows together in thought. "How about a compromise? I go, but stay behind you guys, and if you feel there are too many for me to try and kill, you give the word and I run back to the car?"

"Thank you, baby," I whispered as I hugged him fiercely. His faith in me, and willingness to not only listen to me, but work with me, had me falling even deeper for him.

"Do you have a fax machine?" Mike asked as he opened the bedroom door. I nodded and rattled off the number to my personal fax in the apartment. I heard him give it to someone on the phone before walking back towards the bathroom.

"Let's go kick some ass and rescue people," Gabe

said, breaking the hug and taking my hand. "And to think, a week ago I was living in a convent with cloister nuns."

That stopped me in my tracks. I stared at him for several moments as I thought of how to phrase what I wanted to say. "When this is over, I promise we'll find out what happened with the sisters, okay?"

"Thank you, Cal," he said, squeezing my hand. "It's been on my mind, but we've had so much going on, you know?"

"I'm sorry I didn't think of it sooner," I answered, feeling like a heel.

"Cal, you've got a fax coming in," Beck called out from the living room. I jogged over towards him, Gabe following me. The living room was packed with every demon I'd pretty much ever met, known, or worked with.

"Thanks, Beck," I said, taking the fax from him. Glancing over the schematic, I made note of the exits. Moving over to the counter, I laid out the four pages that made one larger blueprint. "I say we make a diversion here at the front, draw them out. It seems this back area is the best spot to keep captives. We have half the team cover those in case anyone tries to escape."

"Doc's on his way, and everything is set downstairs," Mick informed me as he joined the group. "Are we ready?"

"Yeah, let's do this," Eaton answered as I gathered up the papers. I watched as everyone started towards the elevators, realizing Gabe and I were still in pajama pants. With a wave of my hand, we were in black tactical gear. Gabe let out a yelp of surprise and gave me a look. I shrugged and went to hug him.

"Don't even have to ask my size, do you?" He laughed as he hugged me back. "I'd like a heads up next time; it feels weird."

"Sorry, I'm just so used to doing things that way. Saves time," I replied, kissing him quickly. The next group got on the elevator and went downstairs. I eyed Beck as he watched Mick with a worried look. Did I miss something there?

The ding of the elevator brought me back from my thoughts. The last of us walked onto it, and I pushed the button for the main floor. I put my arm over Gabe's shoulder, proud that he wanted to go in with us, but scared out of my mind for his safety.

CHAPTER 7

About twenty minutes later, we were all piling out of the SUVs about a block away from the old seafood plant. I didn't have much reason to ever come down to this area and was shocked at how many buildings were there, falling apart. Most of the surrounding warehouses and buildings were abandoned, had windows missing, and looked like they hadn't been used in years.

Beck was busy splitting us up into two groups, telling the back group to divide between the two rear exits. They headed out before he turned to the rest of us.

"What did you have in mind for this diversion?" he asked me.

"I'm up for suggestions," I answered with a shrug.

"I was kind of thinking maybe Gabe could give a good scream," he replied with a cringe. "I mean that's something they'd probably want to check out. I figured we give them a few moments to get away from the captives before we rush the place."

"I'm good with screaming." Gabe giggled. I nodded, knowing it wouldn't put Gabe in any additional danger. Beck look relieved as we turned and made our way to the entrance. Gabe took my hand as we jogged over, giving it a good squeeze as if comforting me. The thought almost made me laugh, but instead I was touched by the gesture. He was so much smaller than me, almost fragile at times, but stronger than any man I'd ever been with.

"Alright, you're up, Gabe," Beck informed us as we reached the front doors. Gabe gave him a nod, before letting out a bloodcurdling scream. I just stared at him, wondering where that had come from.

"Stay behind us, baby," I said when he was done. "And please don't ever make that sound again."

"No problem, it bothered me," he replied with a shiver. We waited a few more moments, and then Beck kicked in the door. Most of the wrath demons went in first, then Eaton and Mick. I pulled up the rear with Gabe, charging in after my friends. Immediately, I saw ten halfers that had come towards the front, probably to check out the scream they heard. Mick was the first to start lighting them up.

I turned to check on Gabe before the first wave of halfers got to us, just in time to see him hold out his hands. Skidding to a stop, I was about to scream for him to stop, that there were too many. Before I could, light shot out of his fingers that hit the first halfer. From him, it seemed to jump to the next halfer, then the closest one after him.

It was like how you see lightning react when it hits someone. The light hit them and then branched out, except it only hit halfers instead of everyone. It lasted for only seconds, and then it was like *poof* they were all gone. I stared around, completely dumbfounded at what Gabe had just done. He'd killed them all in the span of few moments without ever touching them.

A thump caught my attention. Spinning around, I saw Gabe hit the ground hard. I raced to his side, dropping to my knees as I realized he was crumpled and out for the count. When I reached for him, I knew he wasn't breathing. I leaned over and listened, but his heart wasn't beating either.

"Gabe? Baby, don't do this to me," I cried, pulling him into my arms. "Fuck! What did you do, baby? Gabe, please, you have to come back."

"Cal, start CPR," Eaton yelled, running towards us. I laid Gabe back down and started breathing into his mouth. By the time I was done, Eaton was there to do compressions.

"Please, baby, I love you. There I said it. You have to come back so you can hear me tell you," I begged, desperate not to lose him. "Gabe, I love you."

"Cal, breathe for him," Eaton growled, and I started blowing into his mouth again. Suddenly, Gabe shook and gasped.

"That's it, baby. Just breathe for me," I cried, my

heart feeling like stone as I pulled him onto my lap and sat my butt on the ground. Relief flooded me as he started to take deep breaths on his own. His eyes fluttered open, and he seemed dazed for a few moments.

"Did you say you love me?" he whispered, staring at me.

"Yes, I love you, baby," I answered, hugging him gently. "You can't *ever* do that to me again. I cannot lose you, Gabe. I love you, you're everything to me."

"I love you too, Cal," he said, smiling up at me. "And I'm starving."

"Fuck! You guys are never boring," Eaton said, standing as he shook his head.

"You can have whatever you want to eat, my little sprite," I told him as I kept crying, more of relief now than grief.

"Don't cry, Cal. I'm fine," Gabe said, reaching up to wipe away my tears.

"No! You're not fine! You stopped breathing, Gabe," I yelled, but then lowered my voice when he winced. "Don't you ever do that to me again, Gabe. Or so help me god, I'll paddle your ass for a week. You can't ever fucking die on me; it would kill me."

"I didn't mean to get them all, it just kind of happened," Gabe replied searching my eyes. "It's not like I have a gauge on this power. I wouldn't have done it if I'd realized it could have taken me away from you."

"Fine, I forgive you. But never again, Gabe," I said firmly, trying to get myself under control. "I love you, baby."

"I love you too," he replied, pulling my head down. I gave in and kissed my little mate. "I'm sorry I scared you."

"Scared doesn't even begin to cover what I felt," I whispered against his lips. I picked him up into my arms as I stood. I turned to Eaton and a few of the wrath demons. "Load someone into the SUV quick, I want to get Gabe home and get him checked out. And then I need to feed him before I fuck him into the mattress."

"Sounds perfect," Gabe purred, squirming in my arms as he started to recover. "I need to feel my hot mate now that he said he loves me."

"I'll say it a million times a day if you never scare me like that again," I replied as I walked us out of the warehouse. I stared into his eyes as I carried him to the closest SUV. "You can't ever leave me, baby."

"I won't, Cal. You're stuck with me forever." He giggled and wiggled his eyebrows at me. Five minutes ago, Gabe's heart wasn't beating and now he was flirting with me? For the love of god, what was I going to do with him?

I hugged him closer and jogged the rest of the way to the car. Opening the back door, I put Gabe into the middle seat before climbing in after him and pulling him on my lap. With a single thought in my head, I waved away our clothes and ran my hands over his body. I needed to inspect every inch of him for myself to make sure he was really okay.

"I need to feel you, Cal." Gabe panted as he moved to straddle my lap. "I want to wipe that look off your face."

Right then, I needed the same thing, but more because I needed to feel that Gabe was alive again. I reached behind him and pulled out the plug, quickly replacing it with my cock. Gabe threw back his head and cried out as I plunged into him. He was absolutely gorgeous.

"Ride me, baby." I hissed, loving the feel of his tight hole massaging my dick. I slid down in the seat and planted my feet for balance. "Show me how much you love me, Gabe."

"Gladly." He moaned as he lifted himself back off of me before impaling himself right away. I grabbed his hips and helped him, thrusting up hard as he came back down. It was like I was a man possessed. But when I remembered that I'd almost lost this, and him, tears ran down my face as I took my sweet mate. Gabe saw, leaning forward to kiss my tears as we made love in the back seat of the SUV. I watched him as he stared into my eyes, giving me his body and soul.

"Come for me, baby," I said softly. As if on cue, Gabe threw back his head and cried out in complete abandonment. It didn't take long for me to follow right after him. I kept thrusting into him, drawing out both our orgasms as his ass clamped down on my cock. As soon as our climaxes ebbed, I pulled him close, wrapping my arms tight around him as he did the same.

"I will never, ever leave you, Cal. I love you too much to ever miss a moment of our lives together," he whispered in my ear as he ran his hands over my shoulders. "We're going to spend centuries loving each other and our children."

"Promise?" I asked, still shaken from what happened earlier.

"I promise, my mate," he replied, kissing my temple. When he moved to climb off of me, I held him to me tighter.

"You're never allowed to remove yourself from my cock. It's the only time I know you're completely safe," I said firmly.

"Okay." Gabe giggled, squirming on my lap. I glanced over when Eaton opened the driver's door.

"Jesus, Cal. He almost died and the first thing you do is bury your cock in his ass?" he asked, chastising me. I felt my face heat up as it sunk in how big of an ass I was. Gabe reached over and smacked Eaton on the shoulder.

"Shut up, Eaton." Gabe growled. "My mate was giving me what I needed, what I asked for."

"Okay, sorry," Eaton said, holding his hands up in surrender. "More people are coming, so you might want to at least cover up."

"Thanks, Eaton," I replied, waving my hand. I dressed Gabe in an over sized t-shirt, and myself in shorts that were pulled down so I didn't have to move him off of me. One of the wrath demons climbed in the back seat with us.

"Oh, it smells like sex in here." Wade groaned, rolling his eyes. "I so need to get laid."

"You can be Cal's feeding tomorrow, but I get to watch." Gabe purred, eyeing Wade over. I gave him a firm slap on the ass, and he quickly turned his gaze to me.

"Don't forget whose cock is in your ass, baby." I growled, feeling possessive. "Or should I show you again on the ride home?"

"I'm finding someone for *you* to play with, Cal." He laughed, smirking at me.

"Right, sorry," I said sheepishly. "I'm a little all

over the place and possessive after what just happened."

Gabe gave me a wink, and leaned forward to whisper in my ear. "Maybe I'll play with your hot ass while he sucks you off."

I groaned as my cock started to fill right back up. Gabe giggled until one of the other wrath demons loaded a survivor in the back and everyone else climbed in. The fun was pretty much over then and with good reason. As Eaton started the SUV, I lifted Gabe off my cock and then spun him on my lap, holding him against my chest.

Several minutes later, we were pulling up in front of the club; we all climbed out and headed in. Some of the other cars arrived as we were walking through the door. I was, of course, carrying Gabe because we might have just had sex, but I wanted to make sure he was really all right. I know, I'm a selfish dick for having sex with him before he got checked out.

Wade brought the survivor from our car in after us, and the guy looked pretty bad. I glanced from him to Gabe to the doc. Could I really make the doc check out Gabe before this guy? A loud whistle got my attention. Looking over, Noah gestured me over, having seen my dilemma.

"I can check him out while the doc helps the other guy," Noah said as I brought Gabe over. "If he doesn't pass the basics, I'll get the doc. Otherwise, he can probably wait for a full workover until the doctor helps the other guys."

"Aren't smart men sexy?" Mike asked me, waggling his eyebrows at me. "And I was simply excited at how hot he looks in scrubs."

"I'll play nurse with you later, Mike." Noah chuckled as I sat Gabe on the table. "What happened?"

I filled him quickly as he used a stethoscope to check out Gabe's heart. I watched, trying to be patient as Noah checked his other vitals.

"He's fine, pulse is normal. I'd recommend that he get an ultrasound of his heart though, just to make sure there's no permanent damage," Noah said when he was finished. "I know a doctor who runs the free clinic I volunteer at who has a portable one and x-ray machine."

"Call him and tell him I'll fund the clinic for two years if he can bring it here ASAP and keep quiet," I told Noah, whose eyes went wide. "I don't care about the cost, Noah. I want to make sure that Gabe's okay, and I'm sure the doc could use the help. We found more captives than we expected."

"I'll call him now," Noah replied, pulling out his phone as he walked away.

"You better always take good care of him, Mike," Gabe said as he took my hand. "He deserves way better than what life has given him."

"I will, Gabe. I'm already falling so hard for him," Mike answered, his eyes never leaving Noah. "After what he went through today, he wouldn't even hear of staying upstairs. As soon as you guys left, he got dressed in scrubs and came down to meet the doc and help. The more I get to know him the more I'm amazed at the man he is."

"I know exactly what you mean," I said, wrapping my arms around Gabe. "As much as I want to spank him for putting himself in such danger and lock him in our room for the rest of his life, I'm amazed at what Gabe did. He knew he could help, so he did without a thought for himself."

"Cal," Gabe whispered, staring up at me with his heart in his eyes. "I love you."

"I love you too, baby," I replied, kissing his sweet, plump lips. "Do something for me?"

"Anything," he said immediately.

"Take my phone and credit card," I replied, pulling my cell and wallet out of my shorts pocket. I handed them to him as he looked at me with a raised eyebrow. "Talk with Mike about what food is around here and will deliver. Make sure to tell them the service entrance; we don't want anyone seeing this. Order enough food for everyone, but make sure to get something the survivors can eat without getting sick. We don't know how long most of them were held."

"I know a pizza/pasta place that delivers, and they have chicken soup on the menu," Mike informed me with a nod.

"Perfect," I said, kissing Gabe before rushing off to get into the mix. I headed straight for the doctor.

"Noah knows a guy who runs a clinic that has a few portable machines," I told him as he was stitching up a mean gash on one man. "Noah's going to get him here to help and bring his equipment."

"That's good, because everyone I've seen so far needs at least an x-ray," the doc answered, never looking up at me. "And I have one who I think needs his spleen removed. I could really use another set of hands."

"Okay, what can I do in the meantime?"

"Try to get the ones coming in cleaned up as best as you can and ask them where it hurts," the doc said after a few moments. "That can give me at least a gauge of who I need to treat first."

"All over it," I replied, hopping into action. I met the next group at the door and gave instructions as I directed traffic. And that's what I did for the next hour until everyone was finally back from the plant and safe. We had a total of eight survivors in various states of need.

"I'm looking for Cal?" a man asked as he came in

the front entrance. He was incredibly good looking, even in older looking sweatpants and shirt.

"I'm Cal," I answered, reaching out for his hand.

"Oh good, I'm Dr. Chad Warner," he said as he shook my hand. "Noah said you needed some help and my portable equipment?"

"Yes, thank you for coming so quickly, Dr. Warner."

"Chad's fine," he replied as he dropped my hand. "He also said this was something we needed to keep from the authorities. I'm not looking to help in anything illegal."

"Not illegal, I assure you," I said, liking that the doctor had scruples. "I will explain everything to you and the situation as soon as everyone's helped. I ask you please just wait until we have that chance and not call anyone. If someone needs to go to the hospital, that's a different story, but otherwise we need to keep this quiet."

He eyed me over for several moments before nodding. "I don't like it, but I trust Noah. If he says everything is on the up and up, I'll wait for the explanation."

"Thank you."

"Don't thank me yet, I'm going to have a lot of questions," he answered me. "But for now, I need help unloading my equipment."

"Beck, bring a few guys over here," I called out, then turned back to Chad. "And we'll talk about my contribution to your clinic after this as well."

"Hold off on that, I'm not a doctor that can be bought off," he replied firmly. "I appreciate the offer, but I want to know what I'm getting into before accepting. Right now, there are people who need help, the rest we can figure out later."

"I understand completely and think it's commendable that you feel that way," I said as Beck and his crew joined us. "Doc needs help unloading equipment, follow his instructions as if they were coming from me."

"Of course," Beck replied then turned to Chad. "Lead the way, doc."

"I brought what I normally have for the mobile clinic, but I have a feeling we might need more supplies," Chad said, glancing around the room. "I might give Noah the keys to the clinic and have you make another run for supplies."

"Whatever you feel is best, doc," Beck answered as they headed to the exit. I went back over by Noah, who was cleaning up another survivor's wounds.

"I like that doctor, he sticks to his values," I said. "He won't accept any money from us until he knows what's going on."

"That's Chad." Noah chuckled. "He was one of the doctors who helped my gram out. He's a great guy and really cares for his patients. That's why I help out at the clinic when I can."

"Think he can handle everything we're about to throw at him?"

"Yeah, I wouldn't have called him if I didn't," Noah replied, pulling off his gloves. "I've known Chad for years. He's smart, really smart, and he can tell we're helping these people, not hurting them. But you have to understand, he's not only got his license to think of, but the clinic as well. So if he freaks or anything, be patient with him, he's putting a lot on the line to help us."

"I won't forget that he is," I said. Noah gave me a nod as he pulled on new gloves and went to the next patient. I went over to Gabe and Mike next as they were setting up food on the closest bar. Gabe immediately turned to get a kiss from me and then went back to work.

It was several hours later when our normal doc told me they were finally done. He asked if there was a place for him to crash for a while, but to wake him if any of the patients roused. Beck took charge of that, giving the doc his spare room and getting some of the demons to situate patients in available beds on the same floor as the doc.

"I believe you owe me an explanation," Chad said

as he pulled off his scrub gear and cap.

"One I will gladly give, but let's get you some food and take this upstairs to my apartment," I replied, leading the way.

"Thank you, I would appreciate that," he answered, following Gabe and I. Grabbing a few of the bags of leftover dinners, I headed to the elevator.

"I think it would be easier for Chad if Noah was here for it too," Gabe said quietly to me.

"As always, you're two steps ahead of me." I chuckled as I waved for Noah and Mike to join us. They met up with us as the elevator opened, and we all got on. We went upstairs and settled down in the living room. Gabe went and reheated some dinners for Chad and Noah, who had yet to eat.

As soon as they had what they needed, I launched into the whole story. Noah jumped in here and there and filled in what he knew from firsthand, glazing over most of the gruesome parts of his capture. When I was done, Chad was finished eating and simply stared at me. He didn't say anything for several minutes, taking it all in.

"So you're… and he's…" he said, pointing at me then Gabe. "It's not exactly something I can ask you to prove."

"On the contrary," I replied, holding out my hand

and calling a ball of fire. Chad gasped, his eyes going wide as I closed my hand and the fire disappeared. Next I waved my hand and changed his dirty sweats into clean scrubs.

"Okay, I believe you," he whispered as he stared down at his clothes.

"Now can you see why involving the authorities wasn't the best option if it could be helped?" I said carefully, watching him for any adverse reaction. Chad turned his gaze to me and nodded. "Thank you for understanding. Now, Noah speaks the world of you and your clinic. I want to talk to you about funding it for the next few years."

"No, not yet, I have questions," he replied, holding up a hand. "Look, I'll keep your secret and what happened to myself. I won't have you thinking you bought my silence here."

"That really wasn't my intention, Chad," I said gently. "Noah trusts you, and I trust him. And after you dropped everything and came to our aid, I simply want to show my appreciation and help ease your burden. I know how charitable organizations run, there's just never enough funding. This is in no way bribe money. I want to make a donation from our business, file the paperwork, claim it on our taxes and everything."

"Okay, I appreciate that," Chad replied, sitting back

against the couch. "But I still have a few questions."

"Ask and if I can answer, I will."

"Noah," he said, turning to the man he knew well. "How did you feel after Cal fed on you? Did it hurt you in any way?"

"No, not at all," Noah replied. "It was the best fucking orgasm I've ever had, and I was totally spent from it but I was fine otherwise. I just slept like the dead, as anyone does after great sex. I never noticed anything the next day or since. You have to take into account what happened to me though, I mean, what I've been recovering from."

"I didn't feel anything wrong after it either," Mike said.

"So you're not like minions of hell stealing souls? You were born this way?" he asked me.

"We can be called to hell if we don't feed and, in a way, die," I answered honestly. "But no, I wasn't conceived in the fires of hell or anything like that. I had parents, though it's not normal for demons to really be all that parently. As soon as I came of age, I was on my own and I never speak with them. Hell is just happy that we're up here getting people to engage in lust, or anger, or whatever other demons there are. But we're not taking away anyone's choices or pushing them into anything. They give into their lust on their own. I'm not sure I really even feel that's a sin, but that's above my pay grade."

"Fair enough," Chad replied, nodding as he wiped his eyes. "Okay, so Gabe is a sprite, which is a type of fairy that can have children even if male and kill these halfer beings?"

"In the short version, but I'd like to think there's more to me than that." Gabe giggled as he snuggled up against my side. "I'm pretty awesome in bed too, I think."

"You definitely are," I purred, leaning over to kiss him.

"Alright then," Chad said, pausing for several moments. "Then I accept any donation you want to give, and if you ever need me or the mobile clinic, I'm more than willing to help."

"Welcome to the Twilight Zone, Chad." Noah laughed, stood and went over to pat the man on the back. "I wouldn't have called if I didn't know these were good people."

"I know that, just give me a little bit to digest all of this." Chad chuckled as he took Noah's hand.

"In the meantime, we have another spare bedroom if you would like to get some rest," I said, standing with Gabe.

"Thanks, Cal. That would be great," he answered,

smiling at me. I had to give it to the good doctor; we just turned what he thought he ever knew upside down, but he took it with grace. I wondered under the same circumstances how I would have reacted. Luckily, I've been alive for centuries, and there wasn't much that really surprised me anymore about the world. Though, I still seemed to find *people* every so often that do.

CHAPTER 8

I woke the next morning to the sounds of someone throwing up their guts. Rolling over, it didn't click with me what was going on until I saw Gabe wasn't in bed with me. Then I was awake and racing to the bathroom. He was sitting on his feet with his head lying on the toilet seat. Without even thinking, I reacted, running out of our room and down the hall to the spare bedroom Chad was in.

"Chad, we need help. It's Gabe, he never got fully checked out last night," I yelled as I burst into his room.

"Shit," he cussed and leapt out of bed to follow me. We flew back to where Gabe was, and Chad immediately knelt next to him.

"I'm fine, just nauseous," Gabe said, wiping his mouth. I turned to wet a washcloth and handed it to Chad. "My stomach hurts, and I feel a little dizzy."

"We haven't loaded back up the equipment yet," Chad replied, looking at me. I nodded and gently lifted Gabe into my arms. He wrapped his arms around my neck as we went to the elevator. The ride down and the walk across the club I was kicking myself for not having done this the night before. Chad pointed to a table by one of his machines. "Lay him down there."

"Baby, were you vomiting blood or anything?" I

asked him as I brushed back a curl from his forehead.

"Nope, just last night's dinner," he replied with a smile. "It's probably just a reaction to all the excitement last night."

"This is going to be cold," Chad informed Gabe, then squirted some jell onto his stomach. I watched as he flipped some switches and grabbed what looked like a large stamp roller. He ran it over Gabe's stomach, watching the monitor. "Holy fucking shit."

"What?" we both asked as I started to freak out.

"Gabe has a uterus," Chad whispered then seemed to snap out of it. "I mean there's no vagina or ovaries, but he has a womb. Gabe, you're pregnant. Wow, that's something I never thought I'd say to a man."

"Really?" Gabe gasped and then looked at me. "We're going to have a baby, Cal. You're going to be a father."

I stared at him with my mouth hanging open as my vision stared to glaze over. And I did what I'm pretty sure any lust demon would have done if he'd heard his male mate was pregnant. I fainted.

* * * *

"Cal? Come on Cal, wake up," Gabe said, smacking

my face gently. I opened my eyes and stared up at him and Chad who were kneeling on either side of me. "You okay?"

"I knew it could happen, but… I mean you really are now… I need a minute," I rambled out, probably not making any sense. Chad chuckled as he stood up and left us alone. Gabe simply smiled down at me.

"You take all the time you need, sweetheart," he said before kissing me gently. "You're not having second thoughts about kids, are you?"

"No, baby," I replied, sitting up and pulling him into my arms. I saw Noah and Mike race off the elevator over Gabe's shoulder, followed by a few of my partners and wrath demons. Chad held up a hand to stop them as he started speaking to them, I'm sure telling them I fainted. Man, I would never live that one down. "I'm happy, Gabe. It's just a lot to take in, sweetheart."

"Tell me about it." He giggled. "You're not the one who's going to carry our baby."

"Good point." I laughed as we stood up. "We have to call Alejandro. Hopefully we can get him here while Chad is here; it would be nice if he knew how to help."

"I agree," Gabe replied as we walked over to the group. We received congratulations, and I got quite a few smirking comments about passing out, but it was all in good fun. "Can someone call Alejandro for us?"

"Yeah, I'll do it," Eaton answered as he stepped away and pulled out his phone.

"Chad, if you don't mind I'd like you to speak with Alejandro. He can fill you in on what will happen with Gabe's pregnancy," I said, having trouble saying that last part.

"You okay there, big guy?" Sark asked, smacking me on the shoulder. I swallowed loudly and nodded. Gabe giggled as he squeezed my hand in support.

"Are you truly with child?" Alejandro asked, appearing out of thin air.

"Fuck." Chad gasped and took a step back, holding his hand over his heart.

"Yeah, that gets even me sometimes," I said, giving him a smile.

"Is this the doctor I am to speak with?" Alejandro said, not looking too pleased about it. "You tested him for being pregnant?"

"He was throwing up this morning and felt nauseous," Chad answered, still looking a little pale. "We thought it might be a side effect of what he did last night with the halfers."

"Gabe wiped out twenty-two of them like nothing at all," Sark said, glancing at me.

"Extraordinary," Alejandro exclaimed, looking

quite pleased. "So you examined his stomach and found he was with child?"

"He has a womb; it's too early to see a baby on the ultrasound," Chad explained.

"If he has one, he's with child. Sprites don't normally have one," Alejandro replied. I felt stupid that Gabe and I were just standing there listening to the exchange.

"He's standing right here," Gabe said, sounding annoyed as he released my hand and crossed his arms over his chest.

"Sorry," they both replied sheepishly.

"Okay, you told us to contact you when he got knocked up and we have," I said, raising an eyebrow.

"Sprites don't have a long pregnancy like humans. Only six weeks to be precise." Alejandro informed us. "So no more sex during his pregnancy."

"What the fuck? Nice of you to leave that out," Gabe yelled, pushing Alejandro. "We just mated; couldn't you have warned us of that one?"

"I don't care about your sex life, sprite. I care for the continuing of our race, we are a dying breed," Alejandro growled, getting right in Gabe's face. I moved in between them, pushing Gabe behind me.

"Do not make choices for us. Gabe is his own

person, and you will tell us everything from now on, not just the parts you want us to know." I informed him, making it clear I wasn't fucking around.

"As you wish," Alejandro replied, backing off. "In my defense, it is in the handbook I gave you."

Chad kept throwing questions at the fae as Gabe and I watched and listened. The more rules and limits Alejandro laid out for Gabe's pregnancy, the less happy Gabe seemed. I wasn't having any of that.

"Doc, can you keep pumping Alejandro for information and tell us the brief version later?" I asked, feeling relief when he gave me a nod. In a flash, I turned, scooped Gabe up into my arms and raced for the elevator. "We are going to celebrate our wonderful news."

"Yeah, great," Gabe whispered so softly I almost couldn't hear him. He wrapped his arms and legs around me, changing how I held him as we got onto the elevator. I swiped my key card and hit the button for our floor. It was then I realized he was shaking as he sniffled.

"Baby, want to tell me what's wrong?" I asked gently, rubbing his back for comfort.

"Nothing, I mean it's just… it's not enough to cry over. I don't know why I'm crying." He sniffled, burying his face in my neck. My heart was crushed when I felt his tears running down my skin.

"We can't always help how we feel, Gabe," I replied as I walked us off the elevator when the doors opened. "Plus you're pregnant, honey. I think a lot of extra hormones come with that."

"I thought we would have more time before this happened, you know? I mean, time without all the crazy shit that's been going on since we met. Just time to be together, learn everything about each other. Now we can't even have sex and have only six weeks to learn how to be parents. And we had like one minute to soak in the news before it's all we can't do this and have to do this," Gabe rambled as I laid him down on our bed and covered his lips with mine.

"One thing at a time, sweetheart," I whispered against his lips. "Yes, we've had nothing but crazy since we've met. But think of how much that showed us about each other. I know more about you after seeing how you reacted in the most dire of circumstances than twenty dates could ever tell me."

He stared up at me for several moments. "That's a good point."

"And we might only have six weeks, but we have a lot of help," I said as I rolled us over so he was straddling my lap. I sat up and bent my knees for him to lean against as I took his face in my hands. "We've got Chad and Noah to help, and Noah will be on premises. We'll order some books, learn as much as we can, and the rest we'll pick up along the way."

"Why are you being so reasonable?" Gabe cried as fresh tears started again. "I'm freaking out and you're calm and being all logical."

"Honey, you were calm when I *fainted* earlier." I chuckled, hugging him close. "I've seen and done a lot over my centuries on this planet, Gabe. I know without a doubt you will be a wonderful parent, and we will love this baby. And that's more important than all the research and time to prep in the world. Chad and Alejandro can handle all the special circumstances while we celebrate our good fortune."

"How? We can't even have sex," he said, leaning back to look into my eyes.

"Baby, there are lots of ways to have fun that don't involve intercourse." I purred, planting small kisses on his neck. "Showing you some other ways to have fun is part of my plan to celebrate."

"Really?" Gabe panted, melting in my arms.

"Oh yeah," I answered, waving away our clothes. Spreading my legs, I rolled us so he was lying on his back. I licked down his neck to his collar bone, and pausing at his perfect nipples. Slowly I took one in my mouth and sucked hard on it while watching his face. "We've not had much time to enjoy the art of foreplay."

"That sounds like fun." He moaned, spreading his legs wide for me. "I like learning new things."

"Right now, I simply want you to feel everything I do to you, baby. I'm going to make you feel so good while I show you just how much I enjoy the man I love," I said before moving to suck on his other nipple.

"I like that, Cal," he replied, squirming under my touch. I ran my hands down his body and started massaging his hips as I let my tongue travel down his firm stomach. I stopped at his belly button and placed open-mouth kisses all around it.

"Our baby is growing in here." I whispered against his skin. "You're going to give us a beautiful baby, Gabe. We're going to love this baby so much and always protect him or her."

"I love you, Cal," Gabe said softly, running his fingers through my hair.

"Good thing, because I'm never, ever letting you go, Gabe," I swore to him before continuing my assault on his senses. Moving down farther, I stopped when Gabe's cock was in front of my mouth. I blew across the plump mushroom head, getting several drops of pre-cum for my efforts. Gabe whimpered as he pulled his knees closer to his chest. "I love this big cock you have, Gabe. It's very, very nice."

"It's all yours, Cal. Only yours," Gabe said, pulling on my possessive side. Giving a growl, I licked along the slit, groaning at the taste of my sweet mate. "This is my first blow job."

"I promise it won't be your last, my love," I replied, then swallowed his cock. Gabe cried out in pleasure as his dick twitched in my mouth before his orgasm hit. I pulled back just enough so I could let his sweet cum travel over my taste buds. Moaning as I kept sucking on him, prolonging his climax as much as I could, I swallowed every drop.

"I came too fast again." Gabe panted as I pulled off his spent dick. I climbed back up him so we were nose to nose.

"I love that you are so hot for me you can't control yourself, Gabe," I told him firmly. "Don't ever doubt that or be embarrassed by it. Besides, you also recover faster than anyone I've ever been with; it's fucking hot."

"Can I do that to you?" he asked, smiling at me widely.

"Any time you want, sweetheart." I chuckled as I rolled on my back and pulled him to me. "But right now, I want to just hold you, if that's okay. I love the feel of you in my arms, especially after you're all sweet and post-orgasm."

"You really are the perfect man, Cal." He purred as he snuggled his face into my neck. "I'm so happy we found each other."

"Me too, sweetheart," I said, wrapping my arms around him tighter. We lay there for several minutes, simply holding each other and giving gentle caresses. "I think we should turn the spare bedroom where Chad slept into the nursery. It's the closest to our room and gets just enough light in for the baby but not too much for nap time during the day."

"That sounds perfect," Gabe replied, running his finger over one of my nipples. "I want to paint it for either sex, not just pink or blue. Maybe like a jungle theme? Paint some animals on the walls and the whole thing."

"I like it, but I can't draw to save my ass."

"I can," Gabe replied. "The sisters taught me how to draw, paint, all of it. I'm actually not half bad."

"How about I'll paint the room a base color and you can go in later and draw everything out. Then we can fill in the colors a little at a time, I don't want you in the paint fumes," I said carefully. "I hope you're ready for me to be crazy overprotective of you, Gabe. Especially now that you're carrying our child."

"I can live with that." He giggled, pinching my nipple hard. I groaned loudly and ran my hand over his ass. "Your nipples really are a hot spot for you, aren't they?"

"Yes," I hissed as he leaned down and sucked on my right one. "I fucking love it when you play with them."

"I'll have to remember that." He purred as he licked one and pinched the other. "Do you know how hot it would be if you got these pierced?"

"Really?" I asked, looking down at him. "You'd like that, would you?"

"Oh yeah," he replied, pushing his hard-on against my hip. "I would play with them all the time."

"Let's go get them done now." I moaned as he kept playing with them. "Anything to make my man happy and playing with me."

"Can we go shopping for the nursery too?" he asked, sitting up and smiling at me. "If I'm only going to be pregnant six weeks, I'm going to start showing soon, and I won't be able to go out in public then."

"Good point," I replied, pouting when he stopped playing with me. "I have one thing I want to ask first."

"Okay," Gabe said, raising an eyebrow at me.

"I really liked when you played with my ass," I told him, feeling my face heat up. "I was thinking maybe we could try putting a butt plug in me, that way you can play with it and no one would know."

"Oh god, that's hot," Gabe moaned, reaching down to stroke my cock. "Will you wear it while we shop and I could tease you?"

"Only if you promise to take care of me when we got back home," I answered, smiling at my eager mate.

"Deal," he said, moving towards the night stand. I watched as he pulled out some lube and one of the plugs I kept to use on my partners. He eagerly moved between my legs and squirted some lube on his fingers. I smiled at him as I pulled my legs to my chest, exposing myself to him fully.

"Touch me, Gabe." I panted as he eyed my hole. He ran his slick fingers over the crack of my ass. It felt so good I started to shake. I groaned as he pushed two fingers in right away, loving the slight burn that came with the overwhelming pleasure. Gabe was watching my face as he wiggled his fingers in my ass. "Oh fuck, baby. That feels so good, give me more."

"You are so gorgeous," Gabe said as he slid in a third finger. "I can't believe I'm so lucky that I get to spend eternity with you."

"I feel the same way," I replied, moving my hips to impale myself on his fingers more.

"Stroke your cock, Cal. I want to see you play with

yourself while I finger your hot ass." Gabe growled as he stroked over my sweet spot. I looked at him with shock as I immediately reached down and wrapped my fingers around my dick. Stroking myself in time with his thrusting fingers, I was getting very close to my climax. "So fucking hot."

"I love you, Gabe," I cried out as my orgasm swam over me. Just hearing that he desired me that much was enough to push me over the edge and had me coming so hard. Stream after stream of my seed shot on my stomach and chest as Gabe kept fucking me with his fingers. After I was spent, he pulled them out and pushed in the plug, getting another low moan out of me.

"I like this in your ass," Gabe said as he wiggled the end of the plug. I groaned as I lowered my legs down to either side of him. In return, he leaned over and licked my cum off my abs.

"Baby, you're going to be the death of me." I hissed, loving the feeling of his tongue on my body.

"Well, I better stop then." He giggled and went to sit up. Growling, I grabbed him before he could get away and rolled us so he was on the bottom. I kissed him fiercely, thrusting my tongue into his mouth and demanding his submission. My perfect mate melted into me, throwing his arms around my neck as he slid his tongue over mine.

"I love you, Gabe," I whispered against his lips, feeling tears form in my eyes. "You are my entire world, baby. I would do anything for you or to make you happy. I hope you know that."

"I do, Cal," he replied, smiling up at me. "And I feel the same way."

Nothing else was left to say; we simply stared at each other for several minutes. And I was glad we were able to have this alone time to just be together and enjoy our happy news. I realized then I would never get my fill of Gabe, always wanting everything he had to give me. And that was perfectly fine with me.

CHAPTER 9

A few hours later, we had already been to one of the tattoo parlors off the strip and gotten my nipples pierced. We'd then headed to one of the home improvement stores, picked out paint, and bought all the supplies. Noah and Mike decided to join us, since they'd looked at the available apartments already and knew which one they wanted. Gabe and I helped them choose nice colors to suit their style.

Before we had headed out, Gabe had found 'Uncle' Sark and 'Uncle' Eaton and informed them they would be joining us. They both gave me a look of confusion, but I merely shrugged and kept walking towards the doors. Sure enough, they followed along, not even groaning when we said we were going to pick out things for the nursery.

Now that we were at a baby store chain, I knew why. Sark and Eaton were totally getting into helping us select items. I wondered if either of them had ever wished for children over their centuries.

"Guys, your cart is almost as filled as ours is." I laughed at them as we were picking out infant-sized clothes.

"Hey, we can spoil our niece or nephew," Eaton replied defensively. I stopped pushing my cart, walked over to them and threw my arms over each of their shoulders.

Pulling them in close together, we shared a quick three-way kiss.

"Thank you for sharing in this with us and giving your support," I said to my two close friends. "It really means a lot to me, and I know Gabe is thrilled."

"I think you should all kiss again," Gabe purred, inserting himself into our circle. "It was fucking hot."

"I'll share a kiss with you and Cal." Sark chuckled as we separated. "I think I'd like that better than Eaton."

"Nope, my lips are for Cal only," Gabe replied as he ran his hand over my ass, pushing on the plug. I groaned and braced a hand on one of the racks as my cock got rock hard.

"What are you two doing?" Noah asked, turning to watch with Mike.

"Since we can't have sex, Cal came up with a few ideas of how we can still have fun," Gabe explained, reaching in the back of my pants and wiggling the plug. That had me grabbing the rack with both hands and panting like a pile of lust-filled goo. "So he let me put in a butt plug before we left, and I get to play with it while we shop, as long as I take care of him when we get home."

"Which is going to be really soon if you don't stop that, Gabe," I growled as he pulled it out a little before letting it pop back in. "Just remember, payback is a bitch."

"Promises, promises." He giggled as he removed his hand. I let go of the rack and turned to face him. Gabe got to me first, running his hands up under my shirt and flicking my new nipple rings. "You said I get to play all I want."

"You do, baby." I moaned, feeling my knees get weak. "They're still so sensitive."

"That's half the fun, lover," he said, tugging gently on one. "I want you so horny and desperate for me that you're begging for me to touch you."

"Gabe, I'm always horny and desperate for you," I replied, covering his hands with mine so he couldn't keep torturing me. "And I'll beg as much as you want, sweetheart."

"Exactly how it should be." He giggled, then pulled his hands out of my shirt and squeezed my cock through my pants. "And we need to make sure you're fed later. I can't have my big lust demon going hungry."

"No, we can't have that." I panted as he kept massaging my dick. "But maybe we should be a little more subtle considering where we are."

"Good point," Gabe said, looking around as he released me. "Just remember I'm far from done teasing you."

"And you just wait until after the baby is born," I

purred, pulling him back against my chest so I could push my erection against his ass. "I'm going to tease and fuck you in every position possible."

"I look forward to it," he replied, pushing his firm butt against me. I groaned again as I released him and joined Mike and Noah. They both chuckled as they held up different options for baby clothes. Needless to say, I was having some difficulty focusing after Gabe's teasing.

"Okay, so we still need to get a crib, changing table, car seat..." Noah informed me, rattling off a long list.

"Wow, that's a lot of stuff," Sark said, looking from their cart to ours. "We already have two full carts. Who knew something so small would need so much stuff?"

"Live and learn, my friend." I chuckled as we made our way to the next aisle. "We've only gotten clothes and some toys thus far."

"I'll take the full cart upfront and tell the checkout lady to hold it all for us," Eaton said as he pushed our cart away. "I'll bring back another empty cart."

"Thanks, Uncle Eaton," Gabe replied with a wink. I watched him walk over to where Noah was looking at bottles and formula. How could I be so full of love for one small sprite?

"You're a lucky man, Cal," Sark said, patting me on the shoulder.

"I am, aren't I?" I replied with a smile. "He's more than I ever thought I could deserve."

"I think Gabe's exactly what you deserve, my friend. You're one of the good guys, Cal," Sark said before pushing his cart and joining the group. I moved over to where my mate was and lifted him into my arms, giving him a deep kiss.

"What was that for?" he asked when I was done. I lowered him back to his feet, smiling at how he still held onto the baby bottles.

"For being you," I answered, taking one of the bottles from him so I could hold his hand.

"We should hold off on formula until we know if the baby will need something special," Noah said. Eaton appeared then with another empty cart, and Noah placed all the bottles and bags into it. Then we picked out some pacifiers, booties, burping rags, and blankies. Next we chose which car seat we liked and then a crib. I totally laughed at how excited Sark got when he found one that played music to help the baby asleep.

"Cal, come look at this," Gabe called out, waving me over. As I got close to him, I saw it was a mobile for over the crib. I wrapped my arm around his shoulders when I realized it was a Tinker Bell mobile with a bunch of fairy friends. "I think our baby should like fairies right away, don't you?"

"It's perfect," I said, taking it from him and putting it in the cart. "We'll have to go online and see if we can find some more fae stuff."

"I want him or her to love demons too though," Gabe replied, scrunching up his eyebrows. "But I'm not sure how to go about that. I mean most of the demon stuff you can buy would scare the crap out of a baby."

"I agree," I said gently, realizing how hard he was trying to not hurt my feelings. "Our baby will just have to love the real demons in their life."

"Without a doubt." Gabe nodded as we moved on to changing tables and playpens. It took us another three carts and half hour, but finally we had everything on Noah's list. He was becoming quite a handy friend to have around. I'd also talked with Mike earlier, who was happy that Noah was smiling so much after what he'd been through. My phone vibrated in my pocket then, and I dropped Gabe's hand at the checkout so I could pull it out.

Nuns are fine, sending a few guys to see with their own eyes, the text message from Beck said. I had asked him last night to check in on the convent where Gabe had grown up.

Good. Ask Sr. Catherine and the others if they would like to fly back with them for a visit with Gabe and see his new home, I texted back.

You got it, Cal, Beck replied seconds later.

"Cal, you might want to look at the total already," Gabe said softly, his glance darting between me and the register. I followed his gaze and saw we'd just crossed over the thousand dollar mark.

"Baby, your man is worth millions," I whispered in his ear, pulling him close. Giving his earlobe a quick nip, I placed a kiss on his neck. "Don't worry about the money, you just keep our baby safe and fed."

"I can do that," he replied, smiling up at me as he wiggled his ass against my groin. I had to bite back a groan as there were people around.

"I'll pull up the SUV," Eaton called out as he finished paying in the other checkout. I chuckled as my two friends, very large lust demons, chatted about everything the store had to offer as they walked to the exit. I bet we were giving the employees at the store something to talk about for weeks.

"Is it the two of you who are expecting?" the lady at the register asked as she scanned items.

"Yes, we're having a baby," Gabe answered with a smile, then I felt him tense up. "Well not us personally, I mean, men can't have babies, of course."

"We found a surrogate that's due in six weeks," I

said, cutting into Gabe's ramble. I felt him relax as I gave his shoulder a squeeze.

"First one?" She chuckled, looking between the two of us.

"Yes, and we're fortunate enough to have a good friend who's a pediatric nurse helping us out," I said, gesturing to Noah who was putting bags back in the cart. "The other two men in the other checkout have been good friends of mine since we were kids."

"I heard them saying they were going to be uncles," she replied, smiling widely. "I can't say we really get so many men shopping together and making a fuss over baby clothes."

"Cal's friends are really excited for us," Gabe said, taking my hand. "Our baby is going to be so loved and spoiled."

"Always nice to have babysitters around," she replied, nodding. "Do you know the sex yet?"

"We're waiting; we want to be surprised," I answered before Gabe could. He gave my hand a slight squeeze of gratitude.

"Decided on a name yet?" she asked as she rang up the last item. I looked down at Gabe who had the same *oh shit* look on his face as I did. She must have seen it because she burst out laughing. "Well, you still have time, but don't wait until the birth. You'll be so overwhelmed, god only knows what you'll come up with."

"Good advice," I said as I handed over my debit card. "We'll have to think about it while we're getting the nursery set up."

After that, I signed the slip, and she wished us luck and thanked us for our purchases. Everyone each took a cart and pushed it outside where Eaton and Sark had pulled up the SUV and helped us load up. We'd bought so much stuff we barely got it all to fit, having to use the third row of seats for our purchases. Mike and I ended up sitting in the middle row with our men on our laps so we could all fit in.

"I'm starving," Gabe announced as we pulled out of the parking lot. "Anyone feel like pizza?"

"Whatever you want, Gabe," I said, kissing his neck. And it was truly how I felt. Whatever Gabe wanted or needed all I ever wanted to do was give it to him.

* * * *

A week later I was down in the club, signing some delivery forms when the front door opened. Glancing up, I saw the wrath demons enter, followed by a few women dressed in habits. *A wrath demon and a nun walk into a sex club*, I thought to myself; it seemed like the beginning to a good joke.

"Thank you so much for coming, sisters," I said as I approached them. "Gabe will be so thrilled you're here."

"He doesn't know we were coming?" one woman asked, raising an eyebrow.

"I wanted it to be a surprise," I answered, extending my hand. "I'm Cal, Gabe's mate."

"I'm Sr. Catherine, and these are Srs. Isabel and Mary," she informed me, gesturing to each of the women. We all shook hands, saying our hellos.

"I'm sure you'd like to see Gabe," I said, gesturing that they follow me to the elevator. All three smiled as soon as I mentioned his name, love shining in their eyes. Moments later we were stepping off the elevator into our apartment. "Gabe, I have a surprise for you."

"If it's more food, I don't want it! I'm getting fat already," Gabe called out from out bedroom. I chuckled at my little mate's response; he wasn't happy that he'd lost his flat stomach and now had a baby bump.

"No food, but make sure you're dressed," I said, realizing he'd be mortified if he walked out here naked to find the sisters here.

"Why would you care if I was..." he replied as he walked into the living room, stopping when he saw who I had with me. "They're all okay?"

"Yes, Gabe, no one was hurt," Sr. Catherine said, stepping towards him. She gasped when she looked Gabe over as he stood in front of them with only pajama pants on.

"We have a surprise for you as well, ladies," I informed them as I went to stand next to Gabe. "Were you ever told what Gabe was when he was left in your care?"

"An orphan fairy," Sister Mary said, staring at Gabe's stomach. "Why does he look pregnant?"

"Because I am," Gabe whispered, glancing from one woman to the next. "I'm a sprite. We have babies with our mates, even if we're male. I guess we're rare."

"Y-You're pregnant?" Sr. Isabel stuttered before her eyes rolled up in her head.

"Oh shit," I said, leaping to catch her in time. I lifted the smaller woman into my arms and then walked over to the couch to lay her down. "I should have seen that one coming considering it was what I did when I found out you were pregnant."

"Maybe we should all sit down," Sister Catherine replied, guiding a pale-looking Sr. Mary to the couch as well. Gabe joined me on the other couch, looking nervous as I wrapped my arm around him. There were several tense moments where everyone stared at each other before we all spoke at once.

"Please, you ladies go first," I said, once we shared a laugh.

"Do you want some water, Sr. Isabel?" Gabe asked when she started to come around. He went to get up to get it for her when she nodded.

"You rest, sweetheart," I said, putting my hand on his knee. "Ladies, would you all like water? We have tea, or coffee?"

"Tea would be wonderful," Sister Catherine answered for all of them. I stood and went to the kitchen to put on some water as they kept talking. "Are you happy here, Gabe? Did I do the right thing?"

"I'm incredibly happy here, sister. I love Cal, and his friends are wonderful," Gabe said.

"But when we knew that we would send you to your mate one day, we didn't know he was a demon," Sr. Catherine replied gently.

"Or a man," Sister Mary added.

"How many women do you know named Cal?" Sr. Catherine asked, clearly chastising her. "We knew Gabe was gay for a while. That never mattered to any of us."

"Cal is a wonderful man, sister. He's kind and loving and generous," Gabe replied. "One of the humans Cal rescued from some bad guys called a doctor he knew to help us when they rescued some other guys, and Cal's funding his clinic for a few years for helping."

"I didn't get any of that, Gabe." Sr. Catherine chuckled. "I've missed your rambling."

"Sorry," Gabe said, taking a deep breath. "A doctor came to our aid, and Cal's way of thanking him is donating enough money to run his free clinic for a couple of years."

"But what about your soul, Gabe?"

"No! You don't get to do that," he exclaimed and jumped out of his seat. "I love Cal; he's the father of my child, Sister Catherine. I was worried about you so he sent men that work for him to check on you and surprise me by having you visit. You can't come into his home and insult him."

"Yes, she can, Gabe," I said gently, walking over to him. I put my hands on his shaking shoulders and looking into his eyes. "She loves you and is worried about you. I'm not upset, nor has she offended me, honey. Believe me, I expected this. But right now, I need for you to please calm down. I'll answer any and all of her questions, okay?"

"No, I love the sisters, but I love you too, Cal. They can't come into our home and look down their noses at you," he replied, shaking his head as tears ran down his cheeks. My poor little mate was having issues with all his hormones and started crying at the drop of a hat.

"They're not being rude, Gabe," I said, leading him back to the couch. "If you walked in and saw what they're seeing, wouldn't you be asking the same thing? I would be."

"Maybe," he answered, wiping his eyes. "I don't like when people assume you're evil; you're so far from evil it's like the north and south pole."

"I'm glad you think so, baby," I said, kissing him quickly as we sat back down. I rubbed my hand over his stomach as I stared at him. "You need to stay calm for the baby, okay? I don't want any undue stress on you or our little guy."

"Or girl," Gabe replied.

"Or girl." I chuckled, hugging him close.

"I think you've just answered all my concerns, Cal," Sr. Catherine said. Turning to face her, I saw all three of them smiling widely. "I don't believe anyone can be evil and worry for Gabe the way you just did."

"I'm glad you feel that way," I replied, smiling back at them. "But I'm still more than willing to answer any of your questions."

"My only questions now are about how Gabe is with child." She chuckled. "I don't think we ever expected to see the man we raised as our own son pregnant."

The tea water whistled then, and I got up and

walked to the kitchen as Gabe started the story of what happened after he left the convent. I got out three cups, tea bags, and poured the water as he kept going. Bringing them back into the living room, I added to Gabe's side of the story where I could. I joined my mate on the couch and took over the story when he got to the halfers. I explained to them that halfers were the demons that their bible talked about.

We told them about Noah and Mike, along with all the other captives that were taken. Of course, we left out the parts about us mating and having hot sex. They were like mothers to Gabe after all. When we were finally done, all three sat there with looks of shock on their faces.

"I have a question now," I said after a few moments. "Why send Gabe out into the world alone to find me like you did?"

"One of the sisters informed me that a couple of men showed up at the convent," Sr. Catherine replied, still looking shaken up. "She said they had deformed faces, hideous scars and asked if we'd ever taken in a child. They set off all of her inner warnings, of course, and she lied to them. After I learned of this, I knew the best thing would be to sneak Gabe out in the middle of the night. Originally, we were going to explain some of this to him before we brought him to you, but given the circumstances, I felt it was better to get him someplace safe."

"Did they come back?" Gabe asked.

"Yes, but I thought I'd led them on a wild goose chase." She sighed, looking very tired. "I gave them some story about a baby showing up years ago that we turned over to DCFS. But it seems they could sense what you were as Cal did. Maybe when they came back they could tell you were no longer there and followed after you. I really don't know."

"Well, now that we all have our answers, I say we move onto the fun," I said, not liking that everyone had gotten so morose. "Would you like to see how far we've gotten with the nursery?"

"I think that is a wonderful idea," she replied, nodding at me that she understood my changing the topic. Gabe got to his feet, rambling with excitement as he told them of all of our plans. Sr. Isabel and Mary followed him into the other room as Sr. Catherine and I hung back.

"You are always welcome here, sister," I told her as she took my arm. "You are family to Gabe, and I would never keep him from you, I hope you know that."

"I do and I appreciate it," she said, patting my arm before walking towards where the others had went. She paused and turned to look at me. "But if you ever hurt him, I will hunt you down and gut you like a fish. Nun or no nun, I love Gabe as if he was my own and I will end anyone that hurts him."

She turned back and continued to walk, leaving me standing in the living room with my jaw hanging open. After a few moments, I started laughing. I really liked her! And more importantly, I respected her for making her point clear to me. Hearing everyone laugh from the nursery I made my way to them, smiling.

CHAPTER 10

The sisters stayed a few days before they had to get back. Gabe and I had a great time with them, and they promised to come back and visit in a few months after the baby was born. Needless to say we spent most of the time in the apartment; I didn't want any more fainting nuns if they saw the club downstairs when it was open. The best part was Eaton stopping by one day.

"Holy mother of nuns," he said, and got right back on the elevator. We all had a good laugh over that one.

The weeks flew by, but we got the nursery finished before Gabe had to go on bed rest for his last trimester. Granted, it was only a two week trimester, but he was being a trooper. I surprised him with an e-reader loaded up with all types of books to keep him entertained. He learned fast, setting up an account and downloading several other books.

I walked in on him masturbating a few times to whatever hot book he was reading. Of course, I was more than willing to help him out and suck on his cock to finish him off. He'd gotten into me about always having a butt plug in that he could play with relentlessly. Most mornings I woke up to my horny mate playing with my nipple rings.

The morning before the six week mark, I awoke to a soaking wet bed. Throwing back the covers, I saw it wasn't blood or urine, which completely confused me.

"I think my water just broke." Gabe panted, wide awake and sitting up against the headboard. "I've had a few contractions I think, but I wasn't sure until just now."

"Noah," I yelled, hopping out of bed. His and Mike's apartment was finished, but they agreed to stay in our guest room until the baby was born. "Call Chad, Gabe's water just broke."

"What?" Noah asked, appearing in our doorway as he wiped his eyes. "Oh shit, okay, you call Chad. I'm going to help Gabe."

"Right, good idea," I said, diving for my cell as Mike raced in the room. I dialed Chad's number and waited for him to answer. "Gabe's water just broke; he said he thinks he's had a few contractions."

"I'm leaving in five, Noah knows what to do, Cal," Chad replied, obviously having been woken up. "Keep him calm and breathing, I'll be there soon."

"Thanks," I said before hanging up and tossing the phone onto the dresser. Going back to the bed, Noah had already pulled off the wet sheets and mattress pad. Mike and I quickly remade the bed, carefully moving Gabe to the other side while we finished up.

"Cal," Gabe screamed as another contraction hit me. "Something's wrong, it hurts too much. This can't be right, I feel like I'm dying."

"Believe it or not, that's normal, Gabe," Noah said calmly. "Just keep breathing like we talked about; Chad's on the way."

"You fucking breathe," Gabe growled as I took his hand. "I'm about to pull a baby out of my ass, literally."

"I know it hurts, honey," I said softly, moving so I was between him and the headboard. I put my legs on either side of him and pulled him to my chest. "And I promise you can beat us all up later, okay? But remember we're here to help and do what we can. I love you, and I'm so proud of you."

"Sorry, Noah," Gabe whispered, calming down once the contraction passed. "It's just *damn*. You read about how bad the pain is and see women on TV, but it's way worse than I could have ever imagined. I don't know how women do this shit. Weaker sex my ass, men couldn't ever do this!"

"I don't know about that." Eaton chuckled as he and Sark walked into the room.

"Have you ever given birth?" Gabe asked very evenly. Sark and Eaton exchanged a look and shook their heads. "Then shut the fuck up and agree with me or I'll shove a football up your goddamn ass and have you push it out!"

"Fair enough," Sark replied, looking pale and swallowing loudly. Eaton nodded like a bobble head doll as I ran my hands over Gabe's arms to soothe him.

"I think it's hot when you get all demanding and growly," I hissed in his ear, giving it a nip. "I could list all the things you can do after you get through this. And just imagine, we're going to have our baby then, honey."

"I know, I know, and I'm excited about that," Gabe said, tilting his neck so he could look up at me. "I just can't put this into words, Cal."

"I know, baby," I replied, kissing along his neck as Noah placed a cool washcloth on his forehead. "I'd gladly trade places with you to not have you in pain. Keep reminding yourself that this will only last a few hours, but we'll have our sweet child forever. And then we can have lots of hot randy sex again."

"Not in front of the baby though." Gabe giggled, then screamed as another contraction hit. My heart was twisting into knots seeing him in this much pain.

"I'm here, Gabe. You're not alone." I whispered, running the washcloth over his forehead. "I'm sorry I can't bare this with you."

"Hey, you're here," he said gently. "That's better than those dads who sit out in waiting rooms and don't even hold their partner's hand."

"Wild horses couldn't keep me away from my mate," I replied, gasping when he screamed again already; the contractions were getting closer together.

"Shit, Chad needs to get here like now," Noah said, looking at me. "I've delivered babies, but not like this. I'd feel much better if Chad was here in case we need to go in."

"Noah, you're scaring me," Gabe whispered, before turning to me. "Is something wrong?"

"No, baby," I replied giving him my best smile. "Your contractions are coming faster, so I'm not thinking you're going to have a long labor."

"I'm cool with that," Gabe said, settling back down against my chest. "I was ready for this to be over as soon as it started."

"I'm here," Chad yelled from the living room, running into our room seconds later with his bag. "How far apart are we?"

Noah filled him in as he put down his bag and pulled out his stethoscope and blood pressure cuff. Chad nodded and went to work checking out Gabe. I realized I was holding my breath the whole time and started breathing again.

"He's ready to push," Chad said, smiling at us. "We're going to try it this way, Gabe. But if the baby gets stuck or isn't moving, I'm going to have to go in."

"Whatever you need to do for the baby," Gabe replied, looking scared.

"He's just warning you, honey," I said gently. "Everything's going to be just fine."

"Help me get a couple of pillows under his lower back," Chad ordered, and I lifted Gabe up so they could be slipped under him. "Okay, Gabe, as soon as you feel ready, push."

"Oh, I'm ready," Gabe said as I helped him sit up more. He screamed as he pushed, going until Chad told him to stop.

"You're doing really well, Gabe," Chad said, checking in between his legs as his hand was on Gabe's stomach. "Should only be two more pushes, you ready?"

Gabe panted and gave a nod before taking a deep breath and pushing again. It lasted several moments before Chad stopped him.

"Okay, I see the head. You still with me, buddy?" Chad asked, smiling up at us. "One, two, three, push!"

Gabe screamed as he gave it all he had, but then suddenly, he wasn't the only one screaming. Chad guided our baby out, who was screaming its lungs out.

"Congratulations, it's a girl," Chad exclaimed, holding up our sweet little girl.

"Oh, Gabe, you did it," I whispered, peppering his face with kisses as I felt tears roll down my cheeks. "I'm so proud of you."

"Cal, she's gorgeous," Gabe cried, clasping his hands with mine. We watched in awe as Chad cleaned her up before wrapping her in a blanket. He walked towards us and gently placed her in Gabe's arms.

"Welcome to parenthood," Chad said as he pulled his hands away. I stared down at our little girl, shocked that we'd made something so precious.

"She has your eyes, sweetheart," I told Gabe when she opened them and looked up at us. Gabe gasped and shook in my arms. "Gabe, what's wrong?"

"S-she's talking… I heard her," he stuttered, his entire body shaking as he panted. I held him tight, exchanging a look with Chad who shrugged. "Cal, I can hear her in my head."

"What?" several of us asked, all eyes on Gabe.

"She's hungry; it's like I saw her wanting to eat in my head," Gabe explained, confusing the shit out of me.

"You just know what she needs, Gabe," Noah said gently as he handed him a bottle of formula. I watched as our baby girl immediately started sucking on the bottle Gabe held to her lips. "It's normal to have that tie to your baby."

"No it's more than that," Gabe replied, staring down at her. "She looks like a Corrie, Cal."

"Yeah, she does," I said, glad that was the name we'd chosen. It had been Sister Catherine's real name before she became a nun. When nuns take their oath, they take on the name of a saint. But when Gabe and I learned it was her real name, we both loved it and knew if we had a girl, we would name her Corrie. I reached to touch her cheek with my right thumb.

"She just said *mine* when you touched her," Gabe whispered. "She knows that we're hers."

"This is extraordinary," Chad said, sitting down on the edge of the bed. "Alejandro told me fae children could communicate with their parents before they can talk, but he wouldn't tell me any more. Is she using words and speaking in your head, Gabe?"

"No, it's more like images and feelings," Gabe answered, looking up at me. "She knows who we are."

"You're our smart girl, aren't you, Corrie?" I asked, staring at her.

"Yes, your name is Corrie," Gabe said to her. "We named you Corrie, sweetheart."

"Does she like it?" I asked, never taking my eyes off of her.

"I think so, I feel that she's happy," he answered,

then groaned. "Cal, you need to take her for a minute."

I moved out from behind him and took Corrie into my arms, in awe at how tiny she was. Glancing over at Gabe, I was scared that he was okay.

"It's okay, Gabe," Chad said gently. "You're going to have some cramping as your body pushes out everything else. Women have a lining in their uterus that gets shed during birth; your body is pushing everything out that's not needed anymore."

"That's just gross." Eaton gagged and turned away as Gabe's body expelled some more of the leftover womb.

"I'm just fine, Corrie. Daddy's okay." Gabe panted, smiling at us as he worked through another cramp. "Cal, you need to relax; she can feel you're worried."

"Kind of hard not to be," I replied, faking a smile for the baby. "Your body's doing freaky things, and our daughter can talk to you mentally."

"Actually, it's not freaky at all," Chad chuckled, "given the circumstances, of course. Women have this after birth, just on a smaller scale."

"You promise he's going to be okay?" I asked Chad, still freaked out that something was wrong.

"I wouldn't lie to you, Cal," he replied gently. "Gabe's going to be just fine. I want him to rest the next couple of days, but after that, he'll be back to normal. No sex until I give him a checkup in a week thought."

"She's ready to go to bed, Cal," Gabe stated as he covered back up. I glanced down, and sure enough, Corrie's eyes were drooping as she stopped eating.

"Well, this might make being a parent easier now that you can hear her." I chuckled as I climbed back into bed next to Gabe.

"I'm exhausted, but I want a shower so bad," Gabe said, giving me his puppy dog eyes and pout lip.

"Doc?" I asked, never taking my eyes off my begging mate. "Can I get him into the bathtub for a bit?"

"As long as you carry him, and he doesn't try to walk," Chad answered with a nod. "We'll watch Corrie while you guys get cleaned up."

"And I'll make up the bed again." Noah chuckled.

"I like the way she feels in my arms," I said, hesitant to hand her over to them.

"You'll get her right back," Chad replied gently as he took her from me. "You're just going to be in the bathroom, Cal."

"I feel the same way," Gabe said, taking my hand before I could say anything. "But the need to be clean is really, really bad."

"Whatever my mate wants." I chuckled, lifting him into my arms as I got out of the bed. I walked us into the bathroom and waved my hand for a warm bubble bath.

"You're so good to me." Gabe sighed as I lowered us into the tub.

"Oh yeah, hot bubble bath after giving birth." I snickered, sitting him down on my lap. "I spoil you rotten."

"It's not just the bath, Cal," he said gently, staring up at me. "It's bringing the sisters out here, and the e-reader, and holding me through the pain."

"I love you, Gabe," I replied, not knowing what else to say. Reaching for a washcloth, I dunked it under the water and started to clean him up. He groaned and opened himself up to me, my cock taking notice. I couldn't help it! Even though my mate had just given birth to our daughter, he was incredibly hot, wet, and in my arms.

"She's the most gorgeous baby ever, isn't she?" Gabe asked, eyes closed as I kept washing him.

"Yeah, she really is," I whispered against his temple. "You did wonderfully, my little mate. I'm so proud of you. I can't imagine going through labor, but you were a real trooper."

"I don't know about that." Gabe giggled and turned on my lap to face me. "I think I scared Eaton and Sark."

"They'll live." I chuckled, remembering the looks on their faces. "I think it was sweet of them to be here for her birth."

"Yeah, you've got great friends," Gabe said, smiling widely.

"They're not just my friends, Gabe," I replied, kissing him quickly. "They came to be there for you too. I think that makes them just as much your friends as mine. I wasn't the one who included them in the shopping or preparing for the nursery; that was all you."

"I liked the idea of Corrie having uncles." Gabe shrugged. "But I'm glad they had fun."

"Me too, baby. Me too," I replied, hugging him close.

* * * *

Several days later I was holding our sweet girl in my arms as Gabe got her bottle ready. Corrie had to be the most well behaved baby on the face of this earth. I knew it helped that she could tell Gabe when she wanted something, and I couldn't help being a little jealous of their connection.

"What's wrong?" I asked Gabe when I saw him staring at us with tears in his eyes.

"She likes being held in your arms best, she feels safe," he whispered, his eyes darting between me and Corrie. "I know it's silly, but I can't help feeling envious."

"I feel the same way that you can hear her in your head," I said honestly. "It's something you share with her that I can't."

"True," Gabe replied, handing me the bottle. I held it to Corrie's lips as I watched Gabe think about what he was going to say next. "It's a blessing, but at the same time, I hear her thoughts like earlier. I'm glad she feels so safe in your arms, and it makes sense. How could you not feel safe wrapping in those huge, muscular guns? I feel safe and loved when you hold me too. It's just, I don't know, hearing that she likes you holding her best kind of hurts. Does that make sense?"

"Of course, but she still likes it when you hold her, right?" I asked, searching his face, tilting my neck. "It doesn't mean she loves you any less."

"That's true," he answered with a nod. "She does like it better when I change her."

"You can always have that job." I chuckled, reaching for him with my other arm. Gabe smiled as he hugged me as Corrie kept sucking on her lunch. "She loves us both and knows we love her, that's all that matters. I can't get hung up on the fact you can hear her. Or you get upset that she feels safer in my arms, okay?"

"You're right, I was just being silly," Gabe whispered against my chest.

"No, you weren't being silly," I said firmly. "I was feeling the same things you were. We just have to remember to see the big picture too."

"Fair enough," Gabe replied with a nod, taking the empty bottle from Corrie. He put it aside before gently lifting her out of my arms to burp her. It was then I noticed how tired Gabe looked.

"Why don't we see if Noah and Mike can babysit for us tonight?" I asked, rubbing his back as he held Corrie against his shoulder. "We've not been out on like a real date, and I think it would be nice to have a night out. We could go have a nice romantic dinner if you want?"

"Really?" Gabe replied, excitement shining in his eyes. "There's that Italian place everyone raves about off the strip. Do you think we could get a reservation on such short notice?"

"Baby, who are you talking to here?" I asked, chuckling. "You go check with Noah and Mike; I'll get us a table."

"Deal," he said, pursing his lips together for a kiss. I gladly gave it to him, smiling as he walked out of the room with Corrie. Pulling out my phone, I called the owner of the restaurant Gabe wanted to go to. He was a frequent guest at our club, and we'd always accommodated his need for a private room. I talked to him for a bit, telling him it was a special occasion. He graciously said he would make room for us at one of his best tables.

I thanked him and hung up, glad I was getting a night out with my man. Next I headed to the elevator and went to the third floor offices. When I got there, I went straight for Eaton's. I knocked before walking in, smiling as my friend was getting a blow job at his desk.

"What's up, Cal?" Eaton asked with a smirk.

"I'm taking Gabe out for an early dinner tonight," I answered, sitting in one of the side chairs so I had a great view of the fun. It reminded me once again how long it had been since I'd been inside my hot mate. I knew he'd gotten the okay from the doc to have sex, but I wanted to give him as much time as he needed. As a result, I was getting hornier and hornier every day.

"I'll keep an eye on the club," he said, giving me a firm nod. "We won't ever let anything happen to our niece."

"I know that, my friend," I replied, giving him a warm smile. "I simply wanted to give you the heads up and get caught up on what's going on."

"Well, Mick still won't leave his apartment." Eaton grunted, signaling he was getting close to coming. He looked down at the twink blowing him. "Jack yourself off, I want us to come together."

I watched the smaller man pull out his own cock

and start stroking it furiously, moaning as he sucked on Eaton. Moments later he cried out as he swallowed Eaton down to the base. I groaned, rubbing my own groin as Eaton held onto the arms of his chair tightly and let loose. Moments later they were both panting and spent, and I was hard as a rock.

"Thank you," Eaton said to the man as he put his spent dick back into his pants. He turned back to me as the smaller man still lay with his head on Eaton's thigh. "Mick won't feed, and we're all taking turns transferring some of our power to him. And Temp is still adjusting to his new circumstances as well."

"Yeah, that was a shock." I laughed, loving that my friend was happy. Though the situation with Mick was disturbing to say the least. It was almost two months since everything went down with Alex, and he looked like the walking dead. "Well, if you need me, I'll be on my cell."

"We'll be fine," Eaton said, smiling at me. "You go have fun with your hot little sprite."

"Oh I will." I chuckled, standing up. I gave him one last wave as I left his office and headed back to the elevator. Realizing I was whistling as I got on, I smiled at how something as simple as going out to dinner with Gabe made me this happy.

CHAPTER 11

"You look fantastic," I said to Gabe quietly as we walked into the restaurant later that night. He'd been fidgeting with his tie the entire ride.

"I've never worn a suit before," Gabe replied, eyeing himself over. "I feel like a kid playing dress up."

"But you're hot; just look at all the people staring," I whispered in his ear, turning him so he could see that almost every eye in the restaurant was on him.

"That doesn't help, Cal," he hissed, turning his gaze away from them. "Now I feel even more self-conscious."

"I'm sorry, I simply was trying to show you how well you fit in," I said. The owner, Giuseppe, saw us then and started in our direction. "It's just you and me tonight, Gabe. And I think you look mouth watering."

"Thanks," he replied, turning bright red. I wrapped my arm around his shoulders as my old friend approached us.

"I was so glad to get your call, Cal," Giuseppe said, hugging me and Gabe. "And congratulations on your mate and new babe."

"Thank you, Giuseppe," I replied, beaming in pride at the hottie on my arm.

"Giuseppe," Gabe said softly, but then the light bulb

went off over his head. "You sent the huge teddy bear that Corrie loves! Thank you so much, she adores it."

"Corrie," Giuseppe replied, stroking his chin, before nodding. "I love it, wonderful name. And I'm glad she likes my gift. It is rare for any of us to have children; our community is buzzing."

"Oh, you're a demon too," Gabe said, shocked. But as always, Gabe was so smart he immediately understood. "You're a gluttony demon. It makes sense. Cal has a sex club, you have a well known Italian restaurant."

"He's hot, smart, and gives you a child." Giuseppe chuckled, shaking his head. "I wish I could find one of my own."

"Yes, but you prefer women," I said firmly, slapping his shoulder. He laughed as he led the way to our table.

"For one as gorgeous as your man, I'd change my mind," Giuseppe stated, wiggling his eyebrows at Gabe. "Cal, if you would permit me, we have some wonderful specials tonight I would love your feedback on. I know you rarely get a chance to visit us, please allow me to show you a wonderful time tonight?"

"By all means," I replied as I pulled out Gabe's chair for him. "I've never had anything here that wasn't delicious and sinful."

"We aim to please," Giuseppe said with a wink as Gabe giggled. He waved our waiter over as I sat down before excusing himself.

"He's a trip." Gabe whispered, smiling widely at me. "It makes sense that most demons would make their home in Vegas."

"Most of the casinos are owned by greed demons," I told him, smirking at his surprised reaction. "Anytime we want a night away or to enjoy anything the casinos have to offer, I have an in there too."

"My man is connected," Gabe purred, taking my hand. I had to bite back a growl and get myself under control. I'd been having enough trouble keeping my hands to myself since he'd put on the suit. Gabe looked stunning in the gray double-breasted, pinstriped suit. I'd chosen a lavender shirt and silk tie to match his eyes. It was no wonder everyone in the place was staring at him with lust; even some of the men who were there with women. He affected everyone the same way; fairies couldn't help it.

"I'm like your personal genie," I said, squeezing his hand as the waiter poured us some red wine. "Ask and I deliver."

"You always do," Gabe replied with a wink. If he kept this up, there was no way I was keeping myself under control until he was ready for sex again. He watched me intently as the waiter finished up and walked away. "I talked to Chad, and I'm cleared. He also informed me that Alejandro said I would only get pregnant every few years. Something about my body letting me know when it was time, and if we weren't ready for another baby, we'd just have to use condoms for that month."

"Well, that's good to know," I said, taking my glass and gulping down some wine. I decided to change the topic before I ended up stripping him naked and fucking him on the table. "Mike's been doing a good job with the plans for the new club."

"Good to hear," Gabe replied, his face falling from his earlier excitement. Had I said something wrong?

"And Noah got accepted to the Vegas medical school," I continued, trying to keep Gabe in the loop of news. "I guess he starts next month, and Chad gave him a glowing recommendation."

"I'm glad, he deserves to be happy after everything he's been through," Gabe said with a nod. Our salads arrived then, and Gabe let go of my hand, not looking at me any longer. I had no idea why his demeanor changed or what to do about it. Was I doing the wrong thing by trying to not push the idea of sex? Chad had warned me that sometimes it took women a while after giving birth to want to have sex again. I was trying to be understanding and supportive.

Dinner went okay, everything was absolutely delicious. But something was missing. Gabe seemed to have shut down and only gave me one word answers. I tried to engage him in any way I could think of, but nothing seemed to work. The harder I pushed, the more he seemed to fold into himself. The ride home we didn't say one word. And when we got into the apartment, he didn't even thank me for dinner and went to get Corrie.

I sat down in the living room with a glass of scotch completely confused. Gabe had told me everything was fine when I'd asked if something was wrong. But he was lying, even if I wouldn't call him out on it. The problem was, I had no clue how to fix it if I didn't know what was broken.

* * * *

The next night I was leaning against the main bar as Beck gave me the rundown of the night's events. He was in mid sentence when he froze, his eyes going wide. I followed his gaze and saw what he was staring at.

"What the fuck?" I growled when I saw Gabe up on one of the elevated stages. He was swinging on one of the poles as one of our regular strippers watched him. My little mate was wearing nothing but a G-string. Before Beck could say anything, I was making my way through the crowds, storming towards my mate.

It took me several minutes to get to him, Gabe oblivious of my approach. As soon as I got to him, I growled at the stripper who immediately got off the stage. I grabbed Gabe by the arm and stared daggers down at him.

"What are you fucking doing without clothes?" I snarled in his face, beyond pissed. Gabe yanked his arm away from me, his face bright red.

"Trying to learn how to be sexy so you'll want me again," he yelled, looking away from me.

"What are you talking about?" I asked, my anger melting and replaced with complete confusion. "I always want you, Gabe."

"You haven't touched me since Corrie was born." He whispered so softly I barely heard him over the music in the club. "I read this article about how sometimes men stop seeing their spouses as sexy once they've had a baby."

"That's not us, Gabe," I said firmly, pulling him into my arms. "I want you so bad I feel like I'm losing my fucking mind."

"Then why did you change the subject last night when I was talking about sex?" Gabe asked, tears in his eyes. "You couldn't talk about something else fast enough."

"I was trying not to push you," I answered, holding him by the shoulders so I could look into his eyes. "I didn't want you to feel pressured. I was trying to wait until you're ready."

"I'm ready, Cal! I've been ready," Gabe said, searching my face. "I thought you didn't find me appealing anymore."

"Does this feel like I don't want you?" I growled, moving his hand over the erection in my pants. "I changed the subject last night because I was afraid I was going to tear off your clothes and fuck you in front of all of those people."

"Okay." Gabe panted, massaging my groin. "I would have liked that."

"You would, huh? Is that what you want, my dirty little sprite?" I purred, moving my hands over his ass. "Do you want me to show you how horny I've been for your sweet ass?"

"Yes," he hissed, pushing his butt into my hands. "I thought if I learned how to strip and give you a show, you wouldn't be able to resist me."

"I think it's hot you were learning to do it for me," I said, choosing my words carefully as I fingered the G-string along the crack of his ass. "But I'm always unable to resist you, Gabe."

"I'm ready for you, Cal," he purred, pulling on my nipple rings through my shirt. I realized what he meant as I ran my hand between his butt cheeks. My little sprite had a plug inside of him already.

"So fucking hot." I groaned, wiggling the plug. "Are you really ready, Gabe? I don't want to push you, baby."

"Would you shut up and fuck me already?" Gabe yelled fiercely, twisting my rings hard. "I'm beyond ready, Cal. If I get any hornier, I'm going to start humping the furniture!"

"Such language from my innocent mate." I gasped playfully and waved away my clothes. "Remember how I told you payback is a bitch, Gabe?"

"Yes," he whimpered, staring up at me with big eyes as he touched my cock. "I'll do whatever you want, Cal. I need you so much. Can you tease me later?"

"Only because you beg so beautifully," I whispered against his lips before kissing him. When we pulled apart, he was panting, his eyes full of need. "Get on your knees, baby, and suck off your mate before he fucks you."

"Gladly," Gabe purred and dropped to his knees. He immediately took the head of my hard cock into his mouth, and I had to hold on to the pole so that I didn't collapse. It didn't take long of him sucking on me before I felt like I was going to blow. I pulled back as I lifted Gabe up under his arms onto his feet. Turning him to face the pole, I molded my body against him as I yanked on his tiny underwear.

"I've been dying to get back into your sweet ass for weeks, baby," I hissed in his ear as I ripped the G-string off of him. He moaned as I pulled out the plug next, barely giving him time to adjust before slamming my cock into his prepared hole. We both groaned loudly as I bottomed out inside of him. "Hang on to the pole, sweetheart. I'm hard and horny for you; this won't last long."

"You recover fast," he purred as he grabbed the pole with both hands and bent over farther for me. I growled my approval, pulling out slowly before thrusting back into him hard. He cried out in delight, meeting my every move. I grabbed his hips as I started to pound into his tight, sweet ass.

"You strip only for me, my love." I grunted as I smacked his ass a few times as I fucked him wildly. "I will fuck you day and night if that's what my sprite wants. Never doubt how sexy I find you, Gabe."

"Please, Cal. Please, I need more," he whimpered, his head falling forward.

"I know what my mate needs," I purred, licking his shoulder as I leaned down. Reaching around him, I stroked his cock in time with my thrusts. I was getting close to coming when I felt Gabe stiffen up.

"I love you," he screamed as his dick shot ropes of pearly white seed over the crowd. We had quite an audience by then, drawn by the essences of a lust demon and fae. I lifted my head and roared out my release as his ass clamped down on my dick. Gabe was still coming as I pushed in and out of him, prolonging both our orgasms. He slumped into my arms as I came back down from my climax.

"Was that what you wanted, Gabe?" I panted, running my hands over his body as I held him up.

"Oh yeah." He giggled, squirming in my arms. My cock took notice and twitched inside of him, causing us both to groan.

"Do you believe me now that I find you sexy and always want you?"

"I'm not sure, you might have to show me again," he replied, giving a yelp as I spanked him again. "Yes, Cal, I know you want me."

"Good, but I'm still going to show you all night and every day for the rest of our lives," I stated firmly as I pulled out of Gabe and lifted him into my arms.

"I look forward to it, my big lust demon," he said, nipping my lower lip. "Have I ever told you how glad I am we have a sex club downstairs from our apartment?"

"No, but I'm pretty sure you just showed me," I answered with a laugh. Gabe giggled as he threw his arms around my neck and hugged me fiercely. I hugged him back, feeling his love and peacefulness that we were okay. We were more than okay, actually, we were great. And I already wanted to fuck him all over again.

I'm a lust demon, what else is there to say?

THE END

ALSO BY JOYEE FLYNN:

Warrior Camp
Love's Deceit
Love's Indecision
Love's Denial

Wolf Harem Series
Second Chance Bite
Spencer's Secret
Dying Assassin (Coming Soon)

Anything Goes Series
Lust & Fae

North American Dragon Series
Dragon Mine

Marius Brothers Series
Micah
Remus
Stefan (Coming Soon)

Hounds of Hell Series
Avoiding Hell's Gates

With Stormy Glenn:

Delta Wolf Series
Chameleon Wolf
Mating Games
Blood Lust

9630069R0011

Made in the USA
Charleston, SC
28 September 2011